CW00449822

HIDDEN IN THE PINES

Also available by Victoria Houston

Lew Ferris Mysteries

Wolf Hollow

Loon Lake Fishing Mysteries

Nonfiction Titles

HIDDEN IN THE PINES

A Lew Ferris Mystery

VICTORIA HOUSTON

CROOKED
LANE

NEW YORK

Copyright © 2023 by Victoria Houston

All rights reserved.

Published in the United States by Crooked Lane Books, an imprint of The Quick Brown Fox & Company LLC.

Crooked Lane Books and its logo are trademarks of The Quick Brown Fox & Company LLC.

Library of Congress Catalog-in-Publication data available upon request.

ISBN (hardcover): 978-1-63910-147-4
ISBN (ebook): 978-1-63910-148-1

Cover design by Nicole Lecht

Printed in the United States.

www.crookedlanebooks.com

Crooked Lane Books
34 West 27th St., 10th Floor
New York, NY 10001

First Edition: January 2023

10 9 8 7 6 5 4 3 2 1

For Mike

There is but one thing of real value—to cultivate truth and justice, and to live without anger, in the midst of lying and unjust men.

—Marcus Aurelius

Prologue

The banging on the front door was so loud it woke the eight-year-old from a deep sleep. She lay still, listening to the gravelly voice coming from the living room. Was that her father? Was her sister Maggie home late again?

Tossing back the light blanket she'd pulled up to keep her cozy in the breezes blowing through the open window, she crept to the bedroom door. Turning the knob slowly so as not to make a sound, she cracked the door open. Now she could see into the living room and also hear better.

Someone had turned on all the lights. She could see her father standing to the right, his back to her. Her mother was on the sofa with her head in her hands. The police officer was talking.

"Dr. Hanson, Mrs. Hanson, I am so sorry to have to tell you folks this, but we had a call—less than an hour ago—and we got there within five minutes. Your daughter was lying on the bank of the Coon River. A fisherman casting in the weeds along there spotted her and called

911. Dr. Hanson, I recognized her right away. She's in my daughter's class.

"I called for an ambulance, and they got there within ten, maybe fifteen minutes. But she was . . . she was gone. She was gone before we got there."

His voice lowered, but the girl could make out words, words she knew were about her sister: ". . . head injury . . . assaulted . . . marks on her neck . . . I had the paramedics take her body to the hospital and called the coroner—"

"No! No—God, no." Her father grabbed the officer's arm. "Keep that horrible man away from her. You hear me? I don't want him taking photos of my daughter. You know the kind of morgue photos that creep takes of women—and shares them with everyone at the bar. No, I won't have it, goddammit. You keep that bastard away from my child. I don't want him touching her."

The police officer backed away, both hands up. "Yes, yes, I understand, but what—"

"I will go to the hospital with you right now. I will arrange for my colleague, Dr. Fieldstone, to do the exam. He can confirm my daughter's death. Isn't that what you need to authorize an official autopsy? But don't you let that creep near my daughter's body or I will sue the bejesus out of you, out of this town—"

"Okay, okay, we can do that," said the officer, sounding doubtful. "I'll call my chief, and if he'll deputize

2

Dr. Fieldstone to be acting coroner, then he can take care of the death certificate."

"Yes, please. If you will do that, then Dr. Fieldstone can call the Wausau Crime Lab to handle the autopsy. *There has to be an autopsy.* I'll pay out of my own pocket if I have to. Look, Officer, that's all I ask."

The girl in the bedroom could hear her father trying to calm himself down.

"Well . . . I . . ."

She could hear hesitation in the police officer's voice.

"Tell you what, Officer," said her father in his most authoritative MD's voice, "all you need to do is say the coroner could not be reached at two in the morning and as a medical professional, Dr. Fieldstone was available to step in and confirm the . . . the situation. Sound okay?"

"Yes, I guess so," said the officer, after a moment. "Will you come with me now?"

"Let me call Fieldstone and ask him to meet us there. I'll be right behind you."

"And me," her mother said. "I have to see—" She didn't finish.

"Alice, you need to stay here with Judith," said her husband.

"She's sleeping—she'll be fine. I. Am. Coming." Her voice had a tone the girl had never heard before.

The front door closed. The room was silent.

* * *

The young girl lay awake until she heard her parents return. It was dawn, too early for her to get up. Again she crept to the door to listen, but all she could hear were snatches of conversation, as her parents were standing farther away in the dining room.

"Camp counselor . . . accident on pontoon . . ."

She crawled back under her blanket and drifted off to sleep. When she got up, her parents were in the kitchen waiting for her.

"We have terrible news, hon," said her mother, her voice breaking. "Your beautiful big sister was killed in a boating accident last night."

Judith stared at her mother, then her father, then said nothing.

She knew that wasn't true.

Chapter One

Fifty years later Judith Hanson still did not know the truth. Fifty years might have gone by, fifty years of no answers, but she had no intention of giving up: at age eight, she had made up her mind to find out what really happened, and she remained determined to find the person—or people—who had killed Maggie Hanson, her big sister.

With that thought in her mind, Judith placed the last of her personal belongings in the leather tote before turning off her computer. A knock on the office door caused her to glance up.

"I'm going to miss you, boss," said Dan, her right hand and assistant manager at the printing firm. The company had tripled in size over the twenty years they had worked together, fielding successes and disasters in tandem.

"Nice of you to say," she said, smiling up at him, "but it's your turn now, and I'm ready to take life easy."

"Yeah, you said you're heading back to your folks' place in Loon Lake for a few months. Then where?"

Her phone rang, and Judith reached for it. "Excuse me, Dan," she told him. "It's Kate, my daughter. I'll catch up with you on my way out."

Judith turned her attention to the phone. "Hey, hon," she said, "I'll have to call you back. Just going out the door for the last time."

"That's why I'm calling, Mom," said Kate. She was in her early thirties now, married, the mother of two young children and not hesitant to speak her mind. "I've thinking about this, and I'm convinced you're making a big mistake. You know going back to the old place always upsets you. When you're there, you're not yourself. And I want you down here with me and the family."

"I know, I know, but it's time I close down the place and put it on the market. Shouldn't take me more than a month or two. Then I'll be down and find a condo near you."

"There's a lovely one for sale right now. Why don't you hire an estate sales firm to clear out the house and a real estate broker to take care of the rest?" She paused for a moment before continuing. "Mom, you should move down here right now. Right now—hear me?"

Judith laughed. "Kate, you've inherited my worst traits—you are way too bossy. Yes, I hear you. Yes, you may be right. But I have to do this."

She could hear an exasperated sigh from her daughter before Kate spoke again. "Okay, then make me one promise, please? Get down here by Christmas."

"That's easy. I absolutely promise to be there for the holidays, maybe even Thanksgiving. Evanston, Illinois, here I come."

"Good. Love you, Mom."

"Love you too."

*   *   *

Judith's marriage, short-lived though it was, had made her a mother. Raising Kate had been an ongoing blessing in her life. That and her work, where she had lucked out with colleagues and challenges that had kept her mind off her mission—most of the time.

Now she was free to explore the few clues she had unearthed as she tried numerous times to find out more about the night Maggie died. It had been impossible to talk about it with her parents, but they were gone now.

Few of the people she'd known growing up still lived in Loon Lake, but she had names and contact information. Her plan was to move into her childhood home, begin the process of closing it down—and reach out to anyone who might have known her sister. It wasn't that she hadn't tried before, but nothing had worked.

Judith knew she was likely to fail again, but she wanted to make one more attempt. After all, she knew plenty of friends who had retired to their hometowns. If she was lucky, she might find someone from Maggie's class or the neighborhood, and who knew? That person just might remember that awful night.

She had another reason to go back, and it was one that couldn't happen in Evanston—she wanted to hunt.

*   *   *

She had been ten when her grandfather insisted she go with him to the shooting range. He had a .22 pistol and showed her how to shoot it. That summer, the two of them spent every Wednesday afternoon practicing at the shooting range.

"You'll be able to protect yourself, and that's important now and when you grow up," he'd said. Judith wasn't sure which she'd enjoyed more—becoming an excellent shot or the time she got to spend with her grandfather.

When she was twelve, he surprised her with a 12-gauge shotgun for her birthday. Bird hunting was his passion, and now he had a friend to go with him. "You're my retriever," he would kid her.

One of her high school friends, a boy named Tom, often tagged along with Judith and her grandfather when they hunted grouse. After her grandfather's death and for the few years they'd stayed in touch after college, Judith and Tom would meet up in the fall for a weekend of grouse hunting.

They were pals, not lovers, though they shared a love of the Wisconsin autumns and their walks though the young aspens where the birds hung out. Her heart would lift with plain and simple happiness as she trekked down the deer trails that ran between the slender white birches; as she inhaled the crisp, clean fall air and strode through the high, bright-green grasses. Those days remained golden in Judith's memory, and she planned to do those walks again when she returned home.

*   *   *

She drove into Loon Lake late that afternoon and stopped by the Loon Lake Market to stock up on basics, as she had left the refrigerator empty on her last visit. Walking out the door after making her purchases, she picked up a copy of the day's *Loon Lake Daily News*.

Once in her mother's kitchen, she put away the groceries, poured herself a glass of white wine, and sat down at the kitchen table to check out the obituaries in the newspaper, hoping none of the people she was hoping to contact had died.

This was not her first look at the obit page—she had checked the paper daily online from her office for years. She was glad to see that no one she knew had passed away. Absent-mindedly, she paged through to the final two pages where job openings were posted.

ADMINISTRATIVE ASSISTANT NEEDED IN MCBRIDE COUNTY SHERIFF'S DEPARTMENT read large block letters. Judith idly looked closer at the requirements: she was definitely overqualified. She was also, she figured, older than whoever they might be expecting to hire. She was also not looking for a job.

That evening, before she went to bed, she pulled the newspaper from the trash and read through the ad once more. A thought had occurred to her: she wondered if such a position would give a person access to local law enforcement records. The ad implied that applicants had to be experienced in data transfer, so, Judith surmised, that would make sense.

She certainly had not planned to go back to work, but to research anything she could find regarding her sister's murder? *Yes.* That was exactly what she wanted to accomplish before leaving Loon Lake.

For fifty years she had lived with knowing, from that late-night conversation she wasn't supposed to have heard, the details the police officer had told her parents, details that described finding a girl's body beaten and possibly sexually assaulted. The police officer had told her parents he believed her sister, Margaret "Maggie" Hanson, had been murdered. The next morning her parents tried to keep the truth from her—but she knew. And she had lived the last fifty years determined not to die before she knew what had really happened and who was responsible. This might be a way to find out. Worth a try.

She set her clock to wake early and call for an interview with the McBride County Sheriff's Department. The person to contact was someone named Dani Wright.

That night Judith slept easy.

Chapter Two

~

"Chief, we have one applicant I really like," said Dani Wright, her voice buoyant. "It's a woman—she's a little older but very experienced with office stuff *and* IT. I emailed you her résumé. Got time to take a look?"

In her new role as the senior administrator in the McBride County Sheriff's Department, Dani was finding herself overwhelmed.

Between the organizational challenges of helping newly elected Sheriff Lewellyn Ferris begin to manage the three towns and six townships the county included and updating the department's IT capabilities while simultaneously handling records requests coming in from across the state of Wisconsin, Dani was floundering, and she knew the responsibilities of the job would only increase. Previously, when Lew had been the police chief of their town, she had had no trouble keeping up with her job, but this involved far more responsibility and far more work.

Dani needed help.

*   *   *

Lew Ferris had joined the Loon Lake Police twenty years earlier and watched the town grow as the paper mill expanded and, more exciting, the Northwoods became even more of a tourist mecca than it had been in the early 1900s. Fishing was a growing sport, as bass tournaments and muskie carnivals and a gourmet appreciation for sautéed walleye drew more and more visitors north in the summertime. Fly-fishing, a favorite sport of Lew's since childhood, was also growing in popularity, partly because more women were now taking it up.

And with all that came crime. Cottages were ransacked during the winter months. Drinking—aka Wisconsin's state sport—made for increasing numbers of car accidents and DUIs, especially over the summer months. Snowmobilers added a new dimension: hundred-year-old-trees do not flinch when hit by large, loud machines. The tree wins; the snowmobiler, depending on their condition, goes to the hospital or to jail.

During Lew Ferris's years on the Loon Lake Police force, she'd learned firsthand how the steadily increasing number of visitors was putting pressure on the small-town police forces attempting to patrol the lakes and rivers and forest lands of the Northwoods. As climate change took its toll farther south, McBride County, home to the town

of Loon Lake, was only going to grow more populated—
and more likely to attract bad actors.

When the longtime sheriff of McBride County had
decided to retire, Lew had struggled with whether or
not to run for his position. She knew it would mean a
heavy schedule that was sure to cut into her moments of
pleasure—her escapes to the trout stream.

Then two things happened. First, a totally unquali-
fied (in her opinion) man who'd been a police officer for
only a few years decided to run for sheriff of McBride
County. In his political ads on TV and in the newspaper, he bragged of having shot "a twelve-point buck"—
as if that were proof he was a skilled lawman. Lew knew
that such a "score" would appeal to some of his fellow
hunters—male, of course—a fact that she found irritating. More irritating was his not-so-subtle suggestion that "a woman really isn't suited to managing law
enforcement."

When Lew got wind of that remark, she began to
drop her reluctance to consider the position.

The second factor that made up her mind was the
realization that she wouldn't be alone in trying to manage the challenges of law enforcement in the region.
Over her years on the force, she had developed resources
and relationships with others in the field. One was
Bruce Peters, an excellent investigator with the Wausau
Crime Lab. Another was Ray Pradt, an expert fishing

guide—and tracker—who could be depended on to be deputized when a criminal investigation required exploring the impossible through the waters and woods surrounding lake country. And not least, her close friend Dr. Paul Osborne, a retired dentist with an expert knowledge of odontology—the science of using teeth and bones to identify corpses and extract DNA—was there to be deputized when she needed him.

One more person had been key to her ongoing success as the chief of the Loon Lake Police, and that was Dani Wright. Dani, once destined to run a beauty salon, had found her career path diverted when Lew stumbled onto the young woman's natural talent: Dani was a born techie. While everyone else in the courthouse setting struggled with internet searches and data transfers, Dani came by it naturally. And discovered along the way that she liked IT better than creating nail art. Not only that—it paid better, much better. Lew knew Dani Wright's expertise made her and the Loon Lake Police Department look good. And she could do even better if she had responsibility countywide. That was tempting.

So when Lew thought over whom she could depend on if elected, she realized that, yes, being sheriff would not be easy. Yes, it would take time away from her beloved hours in the trout stream. But she had the resources she needed: people, experience, and a love for the community she would serve.

"McBride County is not populated by twelve-point bucks," she told the television and newspaper reporters. "McBride County is home to people, people whose lives I value."

And with those words, Lewellyn Ferris had made her bid to be elected sheriff of McBride County.

She'd won. And today was her first day in her new job.

Chapter Three

To keep up with the increased workload, Dani and Lew had designed a new position, one with multiple responsibilities but a simple title: administrative assistant. No sooner had the position been posted than they had seven applicants. Three were young women with whom Dani had gone to school and who seemed to think that just knowing her was enough of an asset to land them the job.

"Nope, no résumé, no interview," Dani had told them.

Of the remaining candidates, two were so limited in their experience with IT that they still used flip phones. Only the last two looked promising, but one more than the other, and Dani gestured to a résumé on the screen in front of her. "Judith Hanson stands out," said Dani. "She has teaching experience, has been a manager—so she must be good with people—and she knows how to use IT."

Lew studied the résumé: the woman had been a manager of marketing for a large printing company and a part-time teacher of cross-country skiing, and she was a native of Loon Lake returning to her roots. Lew was impressed.

"The only thing she doesn't do is hunt and fish."

"Oh, she hunts," said Dani. "She told me she hunts grouse. But no, I don't think she fishes. Can I bring her in for an interview?"

"Of course," said Lew. "Is she the only one?"

"So far," said Dani. "I know what I'm looking for."

Lew smiled to herself. Ever since Dani's promotion, she had taken on a new air of authority, and it looked good on her.

Dani had once aspired to run her own beauty salon, but that was before Lew had stumbled on her natural ability with IT issues during a murder investigation at the local community college. The young woman, once a model of extreme femininity with elaborate makeup, nails, and hair, now appeared less "girly" while at work: her hair still long but tucked neatly into a bun and a marked lack of mascara.

As she was leaving, Dani paused at the door. "Um, Lew?"

"Yes?" Lew looked up from an Excel printout.

"I was wondering . . ."

"Yes?"

"Is, um, Ray seeing anyone?"

Lew tried hard to hide her surprise. "Ray Pradt? Not sure. Why?"

"Just wondering," Dani said, and then disappeared.

Lew shook her head. Dani, of all people to be interested in Ray Pradt: serial womanizer, pot smoker, expert fishing guide, and Lew's secret source of info on the activities of the bad actors living down roads with no fire numbers. Ray Pradt, who at age thirty-two was too good-looking for his own good.

But, she remembered, when she had first met Dani, the young woman had been in a relationship with a young guy who didn't seem able to hold a job for any length of time. He was dark haired, bearded, and cute, which was almost certain to appeal to Dani's interest in all things physically attractive.

Lew never said anything, but she could see the guy was a jerk. Worse yet, he reminded her of her own ex-husband.

Like Dani, she had been young and too impressed with appearances when she met him. She was pregnant with her daughter, Suzanne, when they married, and at the time, he had had a good entry-level job at the Rhinelander paper mill. Life was good that first year. Then her husband started staying out late Friday after his shift at the mill. By the time she realized he was well on his way to becoming an alcoholic, she was expecting their second child. Things did not get better. And the first time he hit her was the last. Even now she applauded her younger self for being brave enough to pick up their two-year-old and a few clothes and walk out that same night. She stayed with her grandfather for three days, then, with his help, rented a small cabin, got a part-time job, and put her daughter in day care. She never looked back. It took her two years to pay her grandfather back, and handing him the final fifty dollars felt better than graduating high school. Still, she did not wish an experience like that on anyone, let alone a good-hearted young woman like Dani Wright.

While Ray might have his drawbacks, he was very good-looking and currently unattached. And of course, more than once, Dani had observed Lew deputize Ray to help track the miscreants who thought they had found the perfect hiding place back in the forest. She knew, too, that he was Lew's secret source for information on the people who thought they were living off the grid.

Dani also would know that Ray's appreciation of home-grown weed was key to his friendships with "people who know people." Lew suspected Dani had figured out that Ray Pradt's misdemeanor file was a cover for the work, invaluable work, he had done when she was chief of the Loon Lake Police Department.

Now that Lew had been elected sheriff, with more responsibilities and covering a larger area, Ray's value had escalated. Dani was a bright young woman; she might have learned the hard way, but Lew figured that these days she knew a good person when she saw him. And foibles aside, Ray was one good guy.

Chapter Four

Lew moved her attention to the sheet in front of her. Besides hiring the assistant, Lew needed to thoroughly know the lay of the land, and to add personnel herself. She had two police chiefs on the county team, but she would need a police chief to take her old job running the Loon Lake Police Department. Of her two existing police chiefs, she was comfortable with Larry Hames, the chief of police for the town of Pelican Shores, a man in his fifties with a solid twenty-plus years behind him. The second chief, Alan Stern, recently appointed by his town board to head up the department for the town of Deer Haven, annoyed her.

He was only three years into working in law enforcement, and he was consistently rude. Rude to her, anyway. Did he have something against women in law enforcement? Or was she overreacting? She needed to find out. She would also like to know more about any politics behind his appointment. Did he owe someone? Or was he someone whose family connections had overridden his lack of qualifications?

She studied the jurisdiction of each town's law enforcement team. It could be confusing. The boundaries of the towns and townships were linked to the shorelines of the lakes and the often-hidden paths of the rivers snaking through the Northwoods. No sooner were maps updated than a logging dam from the late 1800s would crumble and a river or stream would carve a new route, challenging the guidelines for law enforcement.

Lew sighed. Keeping up with the vicissitudes of nature could be as difficult as protecting the people who lived in the Northwoods there from their intended and unintended bad behaviors.

* * *

Shortly before four that afternoon, Lew heard a knock on her office door and looked up. A familiar face appeared, a welcome familiar face.

"Am I interrupting, Lewellyn? Have a minute?"

Dr. Paul Osborne, retired dentist, student of fly-fishing, and the man who warmed Lew's heart, walked across the room to sit down in front of her desk. She saw concern in his eyes.

"You look worried, Doc. Is everything okay?" she asked.

"Right now it is. Just had a phone call from Mallory that she's driving up from Chicago and wants to stay at my place tonight. Apparently she has a client event of some kind that she has to attend here. It came up at the last minute."

Lew stood and walked around her desk to take the chair beside him. She knew the reason behind his concern. Osborne had two adult daughters from his thirty-year marriage to the late Mary Lee. The youngest, Erin, he was close to. Mallory was another story.

Lew knew that Mallory had been the slender, auburn-haired child that Doc's wife had doted on, calling her "Princess M" and treating her like a human Barbie doll with overly frilly clothes and dancing lessons. Mallory had been a very pretty little girl, and the local women's clothing store often asked her to model.

Osborne didn't argue that she was a cute kid, but he happened to think sports, whether soccer, basketball, or fishing, should be taught too.

When he expressed his opinion on this, his wife had refused to argue, simply saying, "Forget it, Paul. Do not expect her to waste time in a boat."

Erin, on the other hand, was an average little kid with a sweet disposition, dark-brown eyes like her dad's, and a mop of white-blond hair that could not be controlled. Since she was not a child who belonged in a television commercial, she got to spend plenty of time with her dad—in the boat, on the ski trail, and hunting. No wonder, Lew thought, she had become a lawyer with a lawyer for a husband and three kids who loved the outdoors.

Mallory had gone into public relations, where, understanding the importance of appearances, she excelled. As much as Osborne admired his eldest's career success, it wasn't until Mallory was going through a difficult divorce and seeing a therapist—shortly after Osborne had been through rehab at the Hazelden Institute because of a drinking problem—that father and daughter had been able to forge a fragile friendship. They knew their relationship was founded on honesty, and the hard part was Osborne's worry that he would somehow sabotage what they had.

The fact that he worried about it made Lew love him even more.

*   *   *

"Mallory's coming here? That's good news, Doc," she said. "She'll be just in time to enjoy those bluegills Ray dropped off. Dinner is at your place tonight, right? To celebrate my first day as sheriff, or did you forget?"

"No, of course not," said Osborne, and his eyes brightened. He glanced around before saying, "When do you move into your own offices?"

Because McBride County was in the midst of building a large new community center to house the sheriff's offices and the county public health department, Lew was still sitting at her old desk in the Loon Lake Police Department. The construction of the new building had been launched a year ago, long before Lew had been elected sheriff, and it was hoped that the new offices for Lew and her staff might open soon.

"Still under construction," said Lew. "They told me yesterday it could be another month or two before my offices will be ready. I'm going to hate losing my good buddies here." She waved toward tall windows at the far end of the room. Twelve feet high, narrow, and sporting glass panes from decades ago, they dated back to the early 1900s, when the Loon Lake Courthouse had been built. Lew loved gazing west across the lawn to the ancient oaks and lilac bushes bordering the entire block. It was a sight that settled her heart on difficult days.

"Oh, come on, you'll have freshly paved Highway 70 to admire," said Osborne, getting to his feet.

"Thank you, Dr. Osborne," said Lew with a grimace. "See you and Mallory later."

* * *

Lew was getting ready to leave for the day when the phone on her desk rang. "A call from attorney Martha Burns. She wants to speak with you, Sheriff Ferris," said Marlaine, on the switchboard. Lew smiled. After working with the woman for years, she knew Marlaine was taking special care to say "Sheriff" and not the familiar "Chief."

"Thank you," said Lew, and took the call.

"Sheriff Ferris?"

"Yes, this is Sheriff Lew Ferris." She had known Martha Burns since she had opened her law office, but this was the first time Lew had spoken to her as sheriff.

"Just a courtesy call," said Martha, speaking crisply as she always did. "I may be filing a lawsuit tomorrow against your Chief Alan Stern of Deer Haven."

When she had finished with her legalese, the lawyer said, "Or you, the McBride County sheriff, can reopen the investigation into this incident, the death of the Knudsens' daughter . . ."

Lew stopped her. "I'm sorry, Martha," she said. "You probably know it's my first day on the job here. I'm not familiar with the incident. Let me review the accident report and—"

"That's the point," said the lawyer, interrupting her. "No accident. The family wants an official autopsy. They do not believe their daughter drowned."

"Like I said . . ." Lew started.

"I heard you. I also know that the coroner for McBride County is known to be incompetent."

"Can't argue that," said Lew in a grim tone. She was well aware of Edward Pecore's shortcomings.

"Check your file," said the lawyer, her voice softening, "and call me in the morning. I would like to hear that the McBride County Sheriff's Department has reopened the investigation into the death of Sharon Knudsen."

*   *   *

Hell of a first day, thought Lew as she packed up her laptop computer and got ready to head out to Osborne's home. She vaguely remembered the drowning accident. It had happened in late spring when she was deep into investigating the murder of her own brother.

Yes, she would have to check the files.

She knew why she had missed news of the drowning. At that time, her beloved brother, Pete, had died unexpectedly; his body was found floating in a lake near a loon nest, which he had been working to protect. A healthy man in his early sixties who had recently remarried after being widowed, he had also been an active environmentalist dedicated to fighting a proposed sulfide mine that threatened to pollute one of the Northwoods' finest rivers. What first appeared to have been a possible heart attack and accidental drowning had turned ugly when it was discovered he had died of blunt-force trauma to his head and shoulders.

Complicating Lew's investigation into the circumstances of his death were the sudden, inexplicable deaths of two more residents of the area. The wealthy landowner who was about to sell land to the sulfide mining group and her twenty-four-year-old son were both found dead under strange circumstances.

Even as she was stricken with grief, Lew had been confronted with the challenges of solving two more murders, and she was mystified by the odd behavior of her newly widowed sister-in-law. At the same time, Lew's niece, her brother's daughter, had arrived home from college. Stunned by her father's death, she was in desperate need of support by her aunt Lew, with whom she had always been close.

So it was understandable that Lew had not taken the time to read the reports of accidents happening in other towns, no matter how close. She refused to feel bad about that. Yes, she had been the chief of police in late May, but at that time she was primarily a grieving sister and the aunt needed by a despondent young woman.

Chapter Five

༄

"I had no idea our client had a connection to the Loon Lake area. I thought he was a Jackson Hole guy," said Mallory between bites as she inhaled three of the bluegills her dad had sautéed for their dinner. "I didn't know until yesterday that he had been a junior counselor at Camp Ashwabagon over on Hemlock Lake. Is that camp still operating, Dad?"

"No, the owners closed it in the late eighties," said Osborne, watching with alarm as Mallory helped herself to more than her share of the bluegills. A look from Lew told him not to worry about it, so he relaxed and answered the question.

"Family vacations changed around then, with people choosing to spend their money taking their kids to Disneyland rather than sending them off for six weeks of summer camp.

"But when Camp Ashwabagon was in its heyday, your grandfather was the dentist for the camp," said Osborne.

"I took over when he retired. Most of the campers came from the Detroit area, some from Chicago." Osborne sighed. "Summer camp—what a gift for a young kid, especially a city kid. But the owners closed the camp and sold off the property."

"That's too bad," said Mallory. "1 loved Girl Scout camp—no ballet lessons." She laughed.

"I was just reading an accident report about a recent drowning on Hemlock Lake," said Lew, joining the conversation. "Doc, did you hear anything about it? It happened in late May when I was too focused on my brother Pete's death to pay much attention to anything happening in the other towns."

"That's right. Hemlock Lake isn't in Loon Lake, is it?" said Mallory. "I always forget it's next door in Deer Haven, but even so, that's only half an hour away. I know because I had to put my client's address in my GPS. I have a meeting there tomorrow afternoon. This client, Matthew Brinkerhoff, told me he inherited the property on Hemlock Lake from his father. And he got it from his father. It's been in the family for generations."

"Did he say where they were from?" asked Osborne. "Hope he's not connected to one of those old Chicago mob families. If I remember right, they owned some land over there. But that was years ago."

Mallory smiled at her dad. She knew he loved to get into the history of mobsters hiding out in the Northwoods.

"Nope. Sorry, Dad, but the Brinkerhoff family is from Detroit, and I'm told there was an old lodge, which Matt tore down and replaced with an elegant contemporary home that's been featured in *Architectural Digest*. Can't wait to see it." She reached for an ear of fresh corn.

"If your client's originally from Detroit and says he spent a few summers at Camp Ashwabagon, then I may have met him," said Osborne between bites of his own sweet corn. "If he knocked out a tooth diving from the dock. I had more than one of those kids who did that. Hemlock Lake has very clear water *and* a lot of rocks. Kids don't look before they leap."

"Check those old files of yours, Dad," said Mallory. "Be fun to know if you were his camp dentist years ago. I find the guy to be amazing. We handle PR for his hedge fund, which specializes in investing in cybersecurity start-ups. He has investors from China, and the business has been skyrocketing in value. Now he has this multi-million-dollar art collection he wants us to promote."

"Is that why you're here?" said Lew.

"I think so. Every time I turn around, Matt has a new idea. But we don't care," said Mallory, chortling with her mouth full. "Right now, as far as we're concerned, anything with the words *Matt Brinkerhoff* attached means money to us. The guy's business acumen is uncanny. And bold.

"It was just over two years ago that he decided to invest in cybersecurity—first through one small start-up, then a couple more—and today his hedge fund is worth six billion!"

"Lewellyn, going back to your question about the drowning," said Osborne, "I'll check with Herm when I see him for coffee at McDonald's in the next day or two. He has a son-in-law who teaches at the high school in Deer Haven.

"If he doesn't know anything, he'll know someone who does."

*   *   *

An hour later, Lew relaxed, feet up, on Osborne's living room sofa while he washed dishes. Mallory was sitting out on the porch swing catching up with emails on her laptop. All the windows were open and the evening breezes whispered of the fall to come. An owl hooted.

Lew pulled the printout of the accident report on the Hemlock Lake drowning from her overnight case. The report had been written by Deer Haven police chief Alan Stern, and the first thing she noticed was that the man couldn't spell. Or maybe he was clumsy on the keyboard. Whatever the issue, the report had been sloppily prepared. Lew made a mental note to tell Stern to have future official reports checked for errors that could raise legal issues.

The facts appeared straightforward: seventeen-year-old Sharon Knudsen had drowned after falling off a personal watercraft, which had hit a submerged log, causing the Jet Ski to become airborne. The report said that the young woman, who had been riding behind the driver, had landed so hard on the water that she was knocked unconscious and drowned before she could be rescued.

The report was signed by the McBride County coroner, Edward Pecore. The coroner's notes said that Pecore had examined the body after it had been pulled ashore, whereupon he had confirmed the drowning.

Great, thought Lew, who was all too familiar with the politically appointed coroner to have any faith in his determinations other than that he could tell when a human wasn't breathing. Beyond that, Pecore, an ex-bartender who was also the brother-in-law of the Loon Lake mayor, had no qualifications for determining cause of death.

Ed Pecore was so consistently incompetent that Lew, during her years as Loon Lake's chief of police, had allowed extra funding for official autopsies whenever there was any question of cause of death.

"Families have a need to know more than what an overserved barfly tells them" was her rebuttal when her decision was challenged. Enough members of the town board knew Pecore's history that her budget requests always passed.

Given Ed Pecore's role in determining the cause of Sharon's death, Lew could see why the Knudsen family might want a more thorough investigation.

The rest of the report was brief and appeared to have been filed with no additional information other than the name of the driver of the personal watercraft: a male, also age seventeen, named Barry Brinkerhoff.

Brinkerhoff?

Lew sat up straight. "Mallory?" She walked out onto the porch. Mallory looked up as she approached. "Is the name Barry Brinkerhoff familiar? Related to your client?"

"Not sure," said Mallory. "I know Matt's married with a family, whom I hope to meet tomorrow. Why?"

Lew shrugged. "Just wondering. The name came up in some paperwork, that's all." She didn't want to bring up the drowning, especially when she didn't know if the Jet Ski driver was related to Mallory's Brinkerhoff or not—but it wasn't that common a name.

Chapter Six

~

The next day Mallory encountered a tall wrought iron gate at the entrance to 4505 Hemlock Lane—the Brinkerhoffs' place. Towering river rock pillars, which had to date from when the property was originally built, likely the late 1800s, anchored the barricade. While the pillars were not unusual, the electric iron gate certainly was.

Whoa, this is the Northwoods of Wisconsin, not Lake Forest, Illinois, thought Mallory. She had yet to meet her client's wife, and since Matt seemed so low-key, if not modest, about his financial success, she wondered if Mrs. Matt Brinkerhoff might be the source of such a pretentious display of wealth. A fortified gate in the Northwoods, where you were lucky to find a paved driveway?

Wondering what lay ahead, Mallory shook her head. Was she about to discover a stone castle with turrets?

"Mallory Osborne," she said into the metal box threatening her car's side mirror. "I'm here at the invitation of Mr. Brinkerhoff."

No one answered, but the iron gate swung open. The drive to the main house was a good half mile long. No castle but a stark glass-walled contemporary structure reminiscent of Frank Lloyd Wright greeted her. Driving up, she saw dozens of cars parked in orderly rows off to the right. Before she could turn down one of the rows, a young man approached to take her car.

After handing over her keys, she followed the paved walkway from the parking area to a pair of oversize screen doors at the entrance to the house. Music and loud, cheery voices could be heard. A party? That was a surprise.

She had been expecting an evening with Matt and his family. She must have misunderstood—or maybe her secretary had made a mistake?

Entering the foyer, she stepped down half a dozen wooden stairs into a deep, wide living room that buzzed with well-dressed people holding drinks as they clustered in front of plump white sofas and white upholstered chairs. No one was sitting.

Slender brass lighting fixtures zigzagged along the perimeter of the beamed ceiling, illuminating a series of colorful paintings that filled the walls. The artworks looked vaguely familiar, making her feel like she'd walked into a museum rather than a home.

Turning away to study the cocktail crowd, Mallory saw no familiar faces nor any sign of her client. She hesitated, for a moment wondering if she could have gotten her directions wrong and be at the wrong house.

"OMG, I don't believe it! *Mallory Osborne!* I saw your name on the guest list, and I couldn't believe it would be one and the same. How the heck *are* you?" A petite woman, her black hair in soft curls around her face and dressed in a black silk tunic over narrow black pants, rushed at Mallory and wrapped her arms around her in a quick hug. Mallory, startled, searched her memory banks, and then she had it—Sarah, whom she hadn't seen since graduate school.

"What a surprise," Mallory said, finding her tongue.

The woman turned to someone standing nearby and said, "We got our graduate degrees in art history together at Northwestern ten years ago. Right, Mallory?"

"Yes, we did, Sarah," said Mallory still startled but recovering. "What are *you* doing here? I was beginning to think I was at the wrong house."

"I know," said Sarah with a grin, "Matt loves to surprise people. He scored, right?"

"He sure did," said Mallory, returning Sarah's hug. "Sarah, this is a long way from New York City. Isn't that where you live?"

"Technically, yes, but I feel like I live here—well, kinda live here at the moment anyway." Sarah linked an arm through Mallory's and pulled her across the room, waving her other arm as she talked. "I'm the curator for the new Brinkerhoff Collection. See my work? Frankenthaler, Ellsworth Kelly, Morris Louis, Jules Olitski, and that's just a few of the artists Matt has purchased for this collection. You name a color-field painter and I've managed to get at least one for the collection here. Did you see the David Smith sculpture when you came in?"

As her old friend talked, Mallory let her eyes roam over the people around them, still hoping to see a familiar face. "That sounds like a lot of money, Sarah. I mean, like millions of dollars. Didn't the Art Institute just acquire a Frankenthaler for millions?"

"Yes, indeed," said Sarah with pride. She leaned forward to whisper, "Got an offer in on a Georgia O'Keeffe right now. Hoping to hear maybe even tonight."

She continued, keeping her voice low. "Matt is not only a connoisseur, but he's very sensitive to value on behalf of his foundation, so he listens to me when I say what we can pay now and how the value of these masterpieces will continue to escalate with time. He understands how to build a legacy, a legacy of national if not international stature."

As she was chatting on about the art, Mallory recalled that Sarah's parents and grandparents had run a small but prestigious art gallery in New York City. Following family tradition, Sarah had been working toward a PhD in art history when they'd met years before.

No doctorate for Mallory. She had been hoping to complete a master's in the field and continue in arts administration. But that was before she'd gotten into the more lucrative world of public relations—no PhD required.

"But enough about me, Mal," said Sarah, using Mallory's nickname from college days. "What brings you here? I didn't have a chance to ask Matt why you were on the invitation list." Her eyes clouded for a moment, as if she might have forgotten something important. But the thought seemed to pass, and she brightened.

"He's been in negotiations all day." Sarah gave a quick glance around the room. "I guess he still is. So tell me, what did you say brings you here?"

"I didn't say, but I will," said Mallory. "I'm with the PR firm that handles Brinkerhoff & Partners. Matt invited me here to see if we might do some PR for his art collection, but I have to say, I wasn't expecting *this*. This is amazing."

Mallory lowered her voice and leaned into Sarah as she said, "I have to confess I thought he was into wildlife art. He told me he spends time in Jackson Hole, so I just assumed . . ."

"That wasn't a bad guess," said Sarah. "Wildlife art is what he was collecting when we met, but that was before I showed him what can be done with wise investing in contemporary art, *if* you have the money . . ."

"Ladies." A cheerful male voice interrupted her. Mallory turned to see Matt Brinkerhoff, drink in hand, smiling at the two of them. "You've met, I see."

"No, not exactly," said Mallory, "Well, a long time ago. Sarah and I know each other from way back. We went through grad school together. Sarah was a graduate fellow when I was working on my master's. And before you say another word, Matt, congratulations. You have an amazing collection. And I've only been in one room. Just phenomenal." She gestured around the room.

Matt grinned. "I know. Great, isn't it? All thanks to Ms. Sarah Hatch, who has exquisite taste, and"—he raised his eyebrows significantly—"along with your connections, Mallory, I expect Brinkerhoff & Partners to soon rank as one of the outstanding tech companies in America. I can read your press release now: *valuing science and the future alongside the art and culture of our past.*"

"Those are my exact words," said a tall, freckle-faced woman with short, curly white-blond hair as she stepped up to stand beside Matt. She had a large bruise coloring her left cheekbone. "Not bad, huh?"

"Oh, gosh, what happened to you?" said Mallory. The second she spoke, she wanted to kick herself for being so rude.

The woman waved one hand and opened her mouth to speak, but before she could say a word, her husband interrupted. "My wife, Alex," said Matt, introducing her to Mallory. "She insists she's my guiding light."

"Don't know about that," said Alex with a slight smile, "I just make sure he spends more on art than cars . . . or guns . . . or . . ."

Mallory found herself waiting to hear if Alex would say *other women*. But she didn't, and Mallory chastised herself again, this time for being unkind to even think such a thing.

"Yeah, I like to hunt," said Matt, as if to explain his wife's reference to guns.

Looking at Mallory, Alex opened her mouth to say something, only to be interrupted again. "Oh, excuse us," said Matt. "This way, Alex. There's someone I want you to meet."

As the couple walked off, Alex turned back to answer Mallory's question, saying, "I got it in my jujitsu class. Thanks for asking."

When the husband and wife had disappeared, Sarah nudged Mallory. "Not bad behavior, considering she just filed for divorce, hey?"

"Are you kidding me?" Mallory knew she looked stunned. She couldn't help it. "Sarah, that's a black eye on that woman."

"I know. She does martial arts. She just told you she got it doing jujitsu."

"Yeah? Well, then, I guess she did." Mallory shrugged. The evening was seeming a little weird.

*　　*　　*

Mallory's firm, Osborne Associates, had been hired six months earlier to work with Brinkerhoff & Partners on building a corporate image. Matt, a native of Detroit, had taken over his family's chain of sporting goods stores, which he'd sold shortly after his father died. A few months later, his financial adviser alerted him to the exploding market in cybersecurity.

Rather than pay a hefty tax bill on the sale, he decided to gamble. He put all his money into a cybersecurity start-up. His timing couldn't have been better, as cybersecurity was suddenly in demand across the country. The bet paid off.

Mallory knew that six months into the cybersecurity universe, Matt had been approached by a Chinese billionaire interested in acquiring his new company. But Matt had a different idea.

Together the two men established a hedge fund dedicated to investing in other cybersecurity start-ups. At the same time, the Chinese partner made it clear he wished to remain anonymous.

Anyone who knew Matt would know that was fine with him—he was more than happy to have his name on their masthead. So in less than two years, Matt Brinkerhoff and his hedge fund were recognized as one of America's top investment teams in the cybersecurity field. His personal income soared from a few million to over four billion annually—which would mean a serious tax bill.

If Matt was a giant in the tech industry, he was one in person too. A six-foot-four, broad-shouldered man with narrow hips and long legs, he had an outsize head. With straight blond hair, flat, shifty hazel eyes, and a square, pale face, he reminded Mallory of a large fish. A gar, to be exact, a bottom-feeder and her least favorite denizen of lake waters.

But she repressed that thought—she knew he would be a lucrative client. Still, Matt Brinkerhoff was a man with a bland face and what seemed like a matching personality, and no amount of money was going to change that. He might be brilliant, but he was not attractive. At least not to her.

*　　*　　*

After Matt walked off, Sarah excused herself to make a beeline for the guest bathroom, which had been designed to accommodate several women at a time, with separate stalls.

When Sarah emerged from her stall, she found Alex applying fresh pats of makeup, which did nothing to hide the bruise from her black eye. "So, Sarah," said Alex in a teasing tone as she snapped her compact closed, "would you say that Matt has a good eye?"

The question caught Sarah off guard. To her, the phrase *good eye* meant someone could spot talent even if it wasn't ballyhooed by the moneyed patrons crowding the art market, someone who recognized art without needing an expert to explain it. That was not Matt Brinkerhoff, and Sarah suspected Alex knew it.

"Uh . . . um . . ." she stammered, then said, "Your husband knows quality."

Alex laughed. "Right. He knows you get what you pay for. Now tell me he doesn't check the price plus the forecast on anticipated increase in value before he buys. Correct?"

Because it seemed that Alex was about to say something disparaging about her husband and Sarah hoped to stay out of such a discussion, she smiled and shrugged and just said, "He knows what he wants."

"Ah. And does he want you?"

If Alex's earlier question had claught Sarah off guard, this one shocked her. Did Alex know that Matt had been hitting on her in subtle but unmistakable ways? Dropping hints and playful pats on her lower back and hips when she wasn't expecting it?

"I'm not a piece of art," said Sarah, gamely going for a joke—she hoped. "Not an item of substantial value to anyone except my husband and our two little ones. You know, my children are just eighteen months and three years old. We have our hands full." She was desperate to change the subject.

Alex laid down her eyebrow pencil. "Well put. But I know the man, and I suggest you take care." She turned to Sarah, who thought she saw tears in the woman's eyes as she said, "Sounds like your family needs you?"

"That's why I'm here. That's why I run my gallery the way I do," said Sarah, bracing herself on the sink with both hands. "My husband is an aspiring artist whose work I believe in, which is why I am willing to support us for as long as it takes for him to be recognized.

"You know, Alex, I am so fortunate that my parents left me the Hatch Gallery. We may be small, but our reputation as one of the most trusted in the world of contemporary art, which is why Matt has chosen to work with me. Bottom line? I'm here because I have a job to do: a job I love for a family I love."

She spoke with the fervor she felt in her heart every time she got on a plane in spite of her reluctance to leave Eric and the kids behind.

"I envy you," said Alex, her voice soft.

The woman packed her makeup into a small purse, then opened the bathroom door to leave. Before walking out, she gave Sarah a long look before saying, "I'm glad we had this talk. Be very careful."

At the door she turned and gestured toward the bruise on her face. "I did not get this from jujitsu," she said.

The bathroom door closed.

Chapter Seven

∽

Sarah rejoined Mallory, only to be interrupted by her client before she had a chance to speak.

"Sarah, Mallory," said Matt, pulling a young man into their midst. "I'd like you to meet my son, Barry. All this will be his someday"—he waved his arm around the room—"assuming he can stay in school, right?"

He raised his drink, almost in a challenge to the tall, skinny, pale-faced teen standing beside him. The boy had his father's blond hair and an acne-studded complexion. It didn't enhance his appearance that he'd inherited the same shifty hazel eyes.

The boy grimaced at his dad's joke.

"Where are you in school?" asked Mallory.

"Um . . . the U . . . y'know, in Madison," said the boy, stammering. He had a sheepish tone.

"He hopes," said his father. The boy shrugged and walked off. Matt smiled at the two women. "He didn't make his grades last semester, but I know all the right people. Trust me, he'll be there in three weeks."

Mallory knew better than to ask more questions. Sarah, too, said nothing. Matt turned his attention to a couple standing nearby and started to walk off before pausing to say, "Sarah, please come with me. I see someone who had a question on the art. You can answer better than I can."

Mallory waited around, studying the paintings and hoping to talk with Matt again, but he had disappeared. At nine, she decided to leave and made plans to call him in the morning. If he had wanted to impress her with his remarkable house and his art, he had. She was ready to pitch a story to the *Wall Street Journal*, but that could wait until the next day.

As she walked toward her car, one of the young men working as a valet stepped in front of her. "Which car is yours, miss?" he asked in a tone more demanding than necessary.

Mallory was startled to see he was wearing a handgun in a holster belted around his waist. *Ah*, she thought, *security. No surprise, I guess.* With millions in art sitting in a glass-walled house in the middle of nowhere, you'd better have security.

"The black BMW is mine."

"Miss, there are four black BMWs parked here—"

"Really?" Another surprise. "Well, the one with the kayak rack on top—unless you have four of those," she said with a chuckle. She pointed to her car, which had been parked farther down the row.

"Got it. I'll grab your keys," he said, and ran off.

*   *   *

Minutes later, she was about to slide into the driver's seat when she felt a hand grab her left arm. "Wait, Mallory, I need your help." Sarah was standing there, her voice low and tense as she spoke.

Mallory moved to stand up, the car door open behind her. "Are you okay?" The expression on Sarah's face was alarming.

"I am right now. I need to know how to reach you if I need help. Do you live very far away?"

"Chicago," said Mallory. "A six-hour drive from here. But I'm staying with my dad here and heading back home tomorrow afternoon. Why?"

"Can we talk in your car?"

"Of course. Get in."

"Thank you," said Sarah, and she jumped in.

Once the car doors were closed, she leaned back and closed her eyes. "Okay." She took a deep breath. "As you well know, I live in New York City, where I own a prestigious art gallery that I inherited from my folks, and I have a husband and two little girls."

"Yes, I do know that." Mallory wondered where this was going.

There was a long pause before Sarah said, "Matt keeps hitting on me. Know what I mean?"

Mallory nodded, hating what she was about to hear.

"I can't do that. I don't care how many millions of dollars he wants to spend with my gallery, I just can't . . ."

A sob escaped, and Mallory patted her shoulder, saying, "We've all been there. Stay strong."

"He hasn't done anything yet, but he touches me, he makes comments. Let's just say I lock my door to the guest room at night."

"Here," said Mallory, pulling a small notebook from her purse. "This is my dad's phone number. His house is a little over twenty minutes from here. I'll talk to him tonight and let him know you may need an excuse to get away. Maybe even tell people you're spending the night with an old friend and use my bedroom at my dad's place. He won't mind."

"Oh-h-h." Sarah exhaled. "This is what I need, kind of an innocent escape route. Thank you!" She hugged Mallory and looked down at the note Mallory handed her. "Dr. Paul Osborne? Is he an MD?"

"He's a retired dentist, and listen, his significant other, who often stays at his place, is a police officer. Her name is Lew Ferris. She's the sheriff for McBride County, which

is just five miles from here. You'll be in good hands."
Mallory gave her friend an encouraging smile. "Life is
never easy, is it?"

"Oh my God, this makes me feel so much better."

"Sarah, remember that class trip we took to the Art
Institute, and I was so confused by the Brâncuşi collection that I was going to flunk the exam?"

"No, I don't remember that. You always seemed so
smart."

"Not that day. You gave me enough background so at
least I passed. Fact is, I owe you."

"Oh good," said Sarah, grinning as she opened the
car door. Again she exhaled. "Off to fight the good fight.
You know, I wouldn't be doing this, but my husband is
an artist who barely makes any money, so my work with
the gallery is our life. I have to be here."

"I understand," said Mallory. "Do not hesitate to call
my dad. I'll talk to him tonight."

* * *

Arriving back at her dad's house, Mallory found her
father and Lew sitting out on the porch swing enjoying
the August moon. "Dad, Lew, you wouldn't believe the
house and the art. There must be thirty, forty million
dollars' worth of paintings sitting over there on Hemlock
Lake. Who would ever expect?"

She paused as she considered whether or not to mention Sarah's worry over the unwanted attention from Matt Brinkerhoff. She stood in the doorway, silent.

"Something on your mind?" asked Osborne. "Leftovers in the fridge if you're hungry."

"No, thank you." She walked onto the porch and sat down across from them. "I got some difficult information from someone I saw at the Brinkerhoffs tonight, and I hope I did the right thing.

"Sarah Hatch, who runs the art gallery that is finding and buying art for the Brinkerhoff Collection, is an old friend of mine from grad school. She's based in New York City, where she also has a family, but flies in almost weekly to work with Matt Brinkerhoff."

"Oh, so if you visit me more, you'll be able to see an old friend and not just your old man?" asked Osborne with a chuckle.

"Isn't that great?" asked Lew, wondering why the news of an old friend visiting regularly appeared to make Mallory unhappy.

"Yes, it is nice," said Mallory, "but more than that. Sarah is very, very worried that Matt Brinkerhoff seems to expect more from her . . . know what I mean?" She looked at them with her eyebrows raised.

"Are you implying what I think you are?" asked Lew. "Because if you are, that can be a criminal offense."

Mallory, toying with an invisible piece of lint on her knee, was quiet for a long moment. She looked up. "I'm sure she knows that, but she's caught, because this man's business is her livelihood."

Mallory's eyes moistened as she went on. "I hope it's okay with you guys, but I told her to call you, Dad, if say she needed to be safe and ask if she could come over and spend a night here with me, even if I'm not here."

"She doesn't have to ask," said Osborne, without hesitation.

"She doesn't even have to call," said Lew. "Tell her where we keep the key so she can get in here whenever she needs to. And be sure to give her my cell number too."

"So that's okay?" Mallory exhaled.

"Come here, sweetheart," said Osborne, getting to his feet and pulling his daughter close. "Mallory, you are precious to me—you and the people you care about. Tell your friend we want her to be safe. Tell her not to hesitate to call or just come if she needs to. Okay?"

"Thank you." Mallory wiped away a tear. She turned to Lew as she got up from her chair. "I met the kid, the one named Barry. Is that who you're interested in?"

"Yes," said Lew. "Apparently he was involved in a Jet Ski accident where someone was killed."

"Oh, hmm . . . Well, all I can say is, based on a comment his father made after he introduced him, he seems like a low-achieving rich kid. I got the impression his old man has the connections and money to get the kid into the university, even if his grades are ridiculous. That's what he implied, anyway."

*   *   *

That evening, as they lay in bed with the windows open, Lew and Osborne could hear the soothing sound of waves lapping against the shoreline. Lew snuggled up against him.

"Doc, any worries you have had about your relationship with Mallory, you can forget. She made one thing clear tonight: she trusts you. She trusts you and loves you. So relax and get some sleep."

Osborne turned toward her, his face nestled in her hair. "Thank you, Lewellyn. You make me feel like a whole human being again. What would I do without you?"

Chapter Eight

Osborne showed up at McDonald's at the usual time and took his usual seat. Ever since he'd retired three years before, he had enjoyed these mornings with his "McDonald's crowd." Some days they were five "old guys" and some days six or seven. Once in a while even Ray Pradt, thirty years younger than most of the crew, showed up to tell—or retell—one of his bad jokes.

Today the table was full. Dick held court for a while with a tale of his neighbor discovering a bear and two cubs on his back deck. Then Harry, still working at the bank, mentioned they were seeing real estate sales that surprised them. "We've had two customers asking for loans on property that is 'off water.' Now why would that be?"

Everyone shook their heads, wondering. It was Rod Steadman who speculated, saying, "Maybe they don't want to be seen. They don't want us going by on our pontoons and looking through their windows, doncha know."

"But why?" That puzzled everyone except Osborne.

"I think you're talking people who don't want to be identified rather than seen," he said. "Maybe they plan to grow weed. Maybe they got something else going that they want to keep off the radar."

He shifted in his seat. "Years ago," he said, "when I was a kid, I heard my dad telling a friend of his that a couple of mobsters up from Chicago were interested in property off the water for just that reason. We all know some things about people never change, right?"

"Right," answered the McDonald's crowd in a chorus.

"Now I have a question," said Osborne, and he told them about Lew's interest in the drowning accident that appeared to involve one of the Brinkerhoffs. "Anyone know anything about their kid? The one who was driving the Jet Ski?"

"My daughter mentioned something," said Herm. Herm, long retired from his position as a manager at the paper mill in Rhinelander, had a daughter living with her family in the nearby town of Deer Haven.

"Think Bob might be familiar with the kid?" Osborne knew that Herm's son-in-law taught science at the high school and coached tennis during the summers. Quite a few of the people with summer homes in the area sent their kids over to his tennis program.

"Let me ask," said Herm, picking up his cell phone. When he got voice mail, he left a message asking Bob to call him back when he was off the tennis courts later that morning. "If he knows anything, I'll have him call you, Doc," said Herm.

Chapter Nine

Lew walked into her office that morning feeling refreshed. She had spent the previous day sorting through her files from her years as chief of the Loon Lake Police Department and tying up all loose ends before setting out to hire her replacement.

Today was to be devoted exclusively to McBride County. First on her list was the meeting with Alan Stern, Deer Haven's chief of police, who was about to be sued by the Knudsen family unless he could supply extenuating circumstances justifying his decision to declare the drowning of their daughter an accidental death.

*   *   *

Chief Stern was a man of modest height and muscular build. Some would call him "small but tough," Lew thought. Watching him as he entered her office and took the chair in front of her desk, she was reminded of a high school wrestler, a guy too small for football but eager to fight.

"Good morning, Alan," said Lew, her tone gracious. "Sorry this has to be our first interaction, but I'm sure we can resolve the issue of the Knudsen accident easily. All that's needed, really, is for you to make a formal request for the body to be exhumed and an official autopsy performed to determine cause of death. The family insists their daughter did not drown but may have suffered other grievous injuries." Sitting back in her chair, Lew gave him a pleasant smile.

"If you don't make that request, the family has to pay for the exhumation and the autopsy, which can cost them well over ten thousand dollars. I see no reason not to have an official cause of death confirmed by the Wausau Crime Lab."

"I disagree, Sheriff Ferris," said Stern, leaning forward in his chair as if he were in charge of the situation. "Coroner Pecore made that determination, and everything I saw at the site confirmed his certification."

"Coroner Pecore is not a medical professional," said Lew, countering and determined to keep her voice pleasant. "He was appointed by his brother-in-law, the mayor of Loon Lake, and he has no medical training whatsoever. His previous professional experience is as a bartender." Lew worked hard to keep from sounding shrill.

She continued. "The Knudsen family has a right to challenge his ruling, and I don't want to see McBride County held responsible for such a serious error. This could be very expensive for the county should they decide to sue, not to mention gravely harmful to the victim's family."

Stern stared at her. "You don't know what you're talking about." He stood up. "I run the Deer Haven Police Department, period. I make the decision."

"So you are prepared for a lawsuit?" asked Lew.

The phone on Lew's desk rang at that moment. She nodded at Stern before picking up the receiver and answering. "Yes?"

"You have a call from Martha Burns, the lawyer for the Knudsen family," said Marlaine, who was on dispatch this morning.

"We're not finished yet," Lew said to Stern while waiting to have the lawyer's call put through. "This is the lawyer of the woman's family." She switched back to the phone when the connection went through. "Hello, Martha. Your office is down the street just a block or so, correct?" After the woman confirmed that it was, Lew said, "Chief Stern is in my office at the moment. Could you run over and join us? Maybe we can handle this easily. Thank you." She put the phone down.

"Alan, would you like a cup of coffee? The Knudsen family's lawyer is on her way over. We'll talk this over together."

Saying nothing, Stern turned his head toward the large windows facing west. The morning sun lit up the lilac bushes guarding the courthouse with the promise of a bright late-summer day.

In less than five minutes, during which Stern continued to sit in grim silence, a knock sounded on Lew's door.

"Come in, Martha," said Lew. A tidy-looking person, Martha was of medium height, with light-brown, naturally curly hair that kept escaping her efforts to push it back behind her ears.

She wore a no-nonsense black pantsuit, the jacket buttoned closed. Even her earrings were minimal: tiny ruby garnets on each ear. Whenever Lew saw her, Martha looked the same, causing Lew to wonder how many black pantsuits she owned.

If she expressed minimal femininity in her dress, she was the same in manner. Martha Burns had a reputation as a well-prepared criminal defense lawyer, a woman who more than held her own against her male competitors.

"Have you met Chief Stern?" Lew asked.

Martha extended a hand and waited. Stern finally responded but remained seated. Martha took the chair beside him.

"I explained that your clients are requesting a formal autopsy from the Wausau Crime Lab at county expense," said Lew. "Chief Stern is reluctant to approve that. I thought you might have some advice or information that could help resolve this."

"Thank you, Sheriff Ferris," said Martha. She turned to Stern. "I have more than advice, Chief Stern. I have a witness to the event."

Stern stared at her. It was clear that this was a surprise to him.

The attorney continued. "Yes, I believe you were at the site, so you may recall seeing a woman out on a paddle-board about, oh, twenty yards down the shoreline? Not too far away."

"There was some old lady bothering the heron. Why? What does that have to do with the price of pigs?"

Lew was taken aback by Stern's rudeness, despite knowing that he lacked basic manners.

Martha gave a soft smile. "Yes, you're correct. She was 'bothering' the great blue heron. With her phone's video camera. She had been there for a good half hour, so she was in the area when the Jet Ski showed up and stopped at the beach there."

Stern sat staring down at his knees while she talked.

"Our witness recognized the boy driving the Jet Ski. She saw him get off, pull his passenger—a young girl— off, and yank at the top of her swimsuit. The girl was pushing him away and crying when he threw her down on the sand.

"I haven't confirmed this detail, but I believe that she may have been the individual who made the 911 call when she saw what was happening. Mrs. Kirsch, our witness, is a retired schoolteacher in her late seventies from Appleton who has a summer cottage on Hemlock Lake. I tell you that because she recognized the boy.

"When she saw a squad car pull up, she assumed the matter would be handled by law enforcement, so she went back to taking pictures of the great blue heron. It wasn't until she watched the footage several days later that she saw more . . ."

Now Stern looked up.

"Yes," said Martha, "what she saw in the background of her video of the heron was that a moment or two before the squad car arrived, the boy had grabbed a rock and smashed it down on the girl's head." Even Stern blinked at this.

"We have the video," the lawyer continued. "Mrs. Kirsch is willing to testify to what she saw, and I think this more than justifies an official autopsy to confirm what the Knudsen family knows: their daughter, Sharon, did not die by drowning." She spaced out the last five words—*did not die by drowning*—with a distinct emphasis.

Anyone other than Stern would look embarrassed, Lew thought, but he kept his face blank.

"All right, Sheriff Ferris," said Stern with a grunt, "I'll put in the request that Pecore's certification be canceled and an official autopsy be carried out by the Wausau Crime Lab."

"I will follow up ASAP," said Lew, "and request an emergency exhumation and official autopsy. With luck, that may be completed later today. I'll keep you posted, Martha. Chief Stern will rescind the certification filed by Mr. Pecore before he leaves my offices." She glanced at Stern who grunted.

"Thank you, Chief Stern," said Martha, getting to her feet. "And thank you, Sheriff Ferris. I know the Knudsens will be relieved to hear this." And she left the room.

*   *   *

A minute later, Stern, saying nothing, walked out of Lew's office. As he passed Dani Wright, who was coming down the hallway, she heard him say under his breath, "Damn women—keep 'em out of law enforcement, dammit."

"Ready for your interview with Judith Hanson?"

"You better believe it," said Lew, setting down the file on Sharon Knudsen's supposed "accident."

Chapter Ten

An older woman with short, straight hair and a pleasant and unadorned face, Judith Hanson struck Lew as quiet and confident. Her résumé had listed her as having been the senior marketing manager for a large printing operation, and Lew sensed an air of authority about her.

"I see that you are originally from Loon Lake but you've lived in Green Bay for years. What brings you back?" asked Lew.

"Well," said the woman with a smile, "I've inherited my family's home, which I love, and the timing is right. You can see from my résumé that I'm retired from corporate life. My plan has always been to return to Loon Lake. I have no husband, and my daughter and her family live in Evanston, just outside of Chicago, so this works for me. I'm not too far from my grandchildren, but I will have my space." Again the soft, confident smile.

Lew felt herself liking the woman. She could see Dani, who was sitting in on the interview, did too. Judith had to be near Doc's age and had a strong work history, and Lew suspected Dani would be happy to work with someone who didn't need a lot of direction.

Dani turned to Lew. "She lives in that wonderful white house with the dark-green trim over by the old South School. I love that house."

"Sure. I know the one you mean," said Lew. "Your parents lived there?"

"Yes, my father was a doctor, a general practitioner, so my sister and I grew up here. I went to high school here, and then off to college."

"But if you're retired, why do you want to take a job like this?" asked Lew. "You are obviously overqualified, for one thing, and—"

"You think I should sit home and crochet?" Judith interrupted with a smile. "I loved my work, but I got tired of the city. Plus staying busy with you and Miss Wright will keep me out of trouble," she said with a light laugh.

"We're not offering a lot of money," Lew pointed out.

"I don't need money; I need to be out and about and doing something I find interesting. I have never worked in law enforcement, and I find it fascinating."

"It is on a good day," said Lew, grinning. "I see you are well versed in technology, and Dani can really use help, as we have a mandate to convert all the county files, some of which date back to the late 1800s."

"So Miss Wright told me. That will be a challenge and quite interesting, I'm sure. Being a native, I'm looking forward to the history we're sure to find."

*   *   *

After asking Judith to take a seat in the conference room, Lew and Dani took all of five minutes to agree to offer her the position. It took less than a minute for Judith to accept.

"When can you start?" asked Lew.

"Whenever," said Judith. "It's nine thirty—how about this afternoon? Dani can show me around, especially your tech setup. I've spent years on Apple computers, so I'll need to adjust to what your department has."

"One more question," said Lew, leaning back in her chair. "Since you grew up here, the fishing capital of the Northwoods, do you fish?"

"I did. As a kid, I fished almost every day with a cane pole," said Judith. "I went out in the boat with my grandfather, or I fished off the bridge over the dam on the Pelican River. But I haven't fished in years. My dad loved to fly-fish up in the UP, and I may still have his old fly rod. I think it's in the garage at the house."

"You might want to unpack it," said Lew, her turn to smile. "Dani, let Judith know what she's let herself in for."

Dani laughed. Seeing the quizzical look on Judith's face, Dani said, "Sheriff Ferris is a fanatic—"

"Not true," said Lew adamantly. "I *enjoy* fly-fishing, I teach fly-fishing, and I use fly-fishing for personal therapy. That's all. I'm not a fanatic. A fanatic is a person who owns a thousand boxes of trout flies. I have only eight hundred and twelve." She gave a sheepish grin.

Nodding, Judith cocked her head to one side. "I understand. Sheriff Ferris, you may run into my father and grandfather when you're out there on the trout stream. I've no doubt they haunt good waters."

When she left the room, Dani and Lew had a hunch she would work out fine.

*   *   *

That night, after Osborne and Lew had enjoyed a late dinner out at her small farmhouse, they walked down to sit by the lake. Their habit was to sit in silence and watch the mother duck round up her teenagers for an early bedtime.

Early in their relationship, after Osborne had asked Lew to marry him the first time, they had settled on a routine that worked for her: two nights at her little farmhouse, including dinner; two nights at his place, including dinner; three nights on their own, though they would have the option of an evening out. Lew loved their life together and apart. She loved her independence even as they grew closer.

"Doc," she had said the third time he proposed, "the answer is no, and you know that."

"I do," he'd said, "but I'll keep asking."

*   *   *

"Dani and I have hired a woman named Judith Hanson to assist Dani," said Lew as the sun was setting over the pointed tops of the balsams on the far side of the pond. "She grew up in Loon Lake and seems to be around your age. Does the name ring a bell?"

"Sure does. Her father, ol' Doc Hanson, was our family physician. I think she's a year or two older than me, Lew. Isn't she retired from somewhere? I'm surprised she's still working."

"I don't think she has to. She's inherited the family home and seems to want to stay involved. She was an executive with a large printing company over in the Fox Valley near Green Bay."

Osborne was quiet for a moment. "I remember that family lost one of their daughters in a boating accident. My dad and his friends talked about it one year at deer camp. There was some gossip on how the car accident was a cover-up of something worse."

Lew sat up straighter. "Really. What does that mean?"

"All I know is what I heard as a kid," said Osborne. "The scandal in Loon Lake at the time was that the coroner in those days was worse even that our friend Pecore. He was known to take photos of the naked bodies of women who had died, whether in accidents or domestic abuse situations, and share the photos with his buddies at the bars later."

"That's disgusting," said Lew. "I can't believe that."

"That was the rumor. My impression from my dad was that friends who had to deal with serious accidents or deaths in their households would go to extremes to keep that creep out of the picture. Could be that's what happened with the Hanson girl."

"Huh. Interesting," said Lew. "I wonder if she'll mention it."

"Has to be a painful memory."

"Are you telling me to mind my own business?"

She got a squeeze on the shoulder.

Chapter Eleven

Walking into her parents' house late that afternoon, Judith paused in the kitchen. She loved how sunlight filled the kitchen. Many of her mother's original Fiesta plates adorned the wooden cabinet, just as they had when she was a teenager. Half a dozen worn cookbooks still stood alongside one another on the shelf over the counter where her mother, who worked at the library, loved to roll out her pastry dough.

Though Judith had had a home of her own for twenty-five years, life had never felt as settled at it did right now. She had married only once, divorced not long after the birth of her daughter, and been a happy, single working mom until Kate had moved on to pursue a career and settle down with a husband and two young children.

Though Judith's own taste had been contemporary when it came to furniture and interior decor, this house felt right even as it reflected her parents' taste. It also reflected a family life built on warmth and a view of the world tempered with humor. Or it had until her sister's unexpected, devastating death. Then it had become a house of sadness.

* * *

Judith looked through her mail. Before leaving her house, she had been to the post office to complete her change of address. She was pleased to find mail forwarded without issue. Ready to change into what would be the work outfit she should wear to the sheriff's department over the coming weeks, she hurried up the stairs to the bedroom level.

She liked looking at the family quilts that still adorned the beds in the three bedrooms, including her own. The oak furniture and the remarkable oak windowsills and doorframes spoke to a past era that she found comforting.

One habit she had picked up since moving back was to pause each evening as she headed off to bed and stop by the door to Maggie's bedroom. She would knock softly, open the door, and whisper, "Good night, big sister."

She knew it was strange behavior, but she didn't hesitate. One of these nights she hoped to say more. She hoped she could tell Maggie she had discovered what had really happened that terrible night and that other people now knew the truth too.

When I find the person who hurt you, if they are still alive, I will make them pay.

But those were words she did not dare speak. Judith knew better. If she had learned anything in life, it was to keep plans secret until you could make them happen.

Don't say it out loud, she would think to herself. *Don't jinx it.*

Then she would close Maggie's door and go off to bed.

Chapter Twelve

Thursday morning Lew arrived in her office at six thirty, only to find she was not the earliest arrival. She could smell coffee brewing.

"Hope you don't mind," said Judith as Lew walked in, "but I went ahead and made coffee. I hope it isn't too strong."

"Strong works," said Lew, watching as Judith filled one of the mugs sitting on the small table beside the coffeemaker and held it out. Lew took a sip. "Tastes great. Thank you."

"Four scoops," said Judith. "I have a question, Sheriff Ferris—"

"Before you say more," said Lew, interrupting her, "we're going to be working side by side, so please, unless we're in public for a press conference or a county board meeting, call me Lew. That's more comfortable for me."

"Agreed," said Judith. "But if you don't mind, I'm a formal Judith, not Judy. Have been since childhood."

"You don't look like a Judy."

Both women grinned.

"Okay, now your question, Judith," Lew said.

"As I was leaving yesterday, Dani asked me to check with 'the Wausau boys' for a file on a recent accident. Those were her exact words, and she seemed to be in a hurry, so I didn't ask her who the Wausau boys are. Are they people I should know? Like support staff here in the building? I'm sorry now I didn't think to ask her at the time, because I think she's coming in late this morning."

"Yes, she'll be late," said Lew. "Thursday mornings Dani has her hair done."

Judith raised an eyebrow. "Really? We're allowed to take time off to get our hair done?" In all her years of managing people, Judith had never heard of such a thing.

"Let me explain," said Lew. "Dani was in the health-and-beauty program at our local community college and heading in the direction of opening her own beauty salon when I discovered she had a natural talent for IT work. At the time, she needed a part-time job, so I hired her on an interim basis to help out with an investigation the Loon Lake Police Department was involved in.

"So I changed her life. In order to get her on board full-time, I agreed to be flexible when it comes to taking time off for her personal beauty regimen. Believe me, she's worth it, and she does not abuse the privilege. You'll see."

"I understand," said Judith. "And if a woman feels she looks good, she does good. Right?" They gave each other a thumbs-up.

"Wausau boys refers to the Wausau Crime Lab," said Lew. "Someone started calling them the Wausau boys years ago, and it's stuck, even though there are many good women working there these days."

She went on to explain more. "The crime lab assists this county, our three police departments, and other districts similar to ours here in the northern part of the state with criminal investigations. That includes any autopsies required when a death occurs under unknown circumstances. This is critical, as the position of county coroner is by appointment and the individual does not have to be a medical professional."

Lew wanted to add *nor do they need to be sober*, but she decided to say nothing. For the moment. Then she changed her mind.

"The accident report Dani asked you to locate involves a serious situation that happened recently. A young couple were in an apparent accident involving a Jet Ski. Our coroner, Edward Pecore, certified drowning as the cause of a young woman's death. Her family is threatening to sue the county if the Deer Haven police chief doesn't overrule the coroner and request an official autopsy from the Wausau Crime Lab."

"Do they have the grounds to do that?" asked Judith.

"Yes, they do. Pecore was appointed to his position by his sister's husband, the Loon Lake mayor, in spite of the

75

fact he is a serious alcoholic. The man's entire career has been spent behind and in front of a bar."

"This is hard to believe," said Judith, frowning.

Lew leveled a look at her. "Didn't you tell me you grew up here?"

Judith nodded in agreement.

"Well, welcome to small-town politics."

"How often are serious mistakes made by that man?" Judith asked.

"I keep an eye on it. You'll be meeting Dr. Paul Osborne, whom we all call Doc. Doc is a retired dentist, but he specialized in and continues to study forensic odontology, which is the scientific study of diseases of the teeth. Forensic odontologists often assist medical examiners, as they're skilled in working with skeletal remains.

"Given teeth are still the best way to identify dead bodies and excellent sources of DNA, I deputize Dr. Osborne to be our acting coroner when a trusted source is needed for a death certificate, especially if a referral to the Wausau Crime Lab is likely to be needed. I have no use for drunks, and Pecore knows it. The Wausau boys know it, and now you know it."

Lew gave Judith a friendly pat on the shoulder. "Hey, Judith, welcome to the McBride County Sheriff's Department."

Judith frowned. "Does this mean the accident report I'm requesting may have been made in error?"

Lew inhaled before answering. "Without doubt. Based on a meeting I had yesterday with the chief of the Deer Haven Police and Martha Burns, a lawyer for the Knudsen family, the parents of the young girl who died, that accident report is likely to be rescinded in lieu of a felony charge of physical assault. I need to see the report from the autopsy. I requested an emergency exhumation and autopsy yesterday in order to make a final decision on what we do next on this case. Late last night I received a text that the crime lab was able to fit the autopsy into their schedule late yesterday so the report should arrive sometime today. Sooner rather than later, I hope."

"This is so alarming," said Judith. "I worry that Dani trusted me with too much."

"I doubt that," said Lew. "Dani probably asked you to check on the report because she thinks you have more experience handling those guys than she does. The director is a man who can be inexcusably rude when dealing with women."

Judith raised an eyebrow again.

"Don't ask." Lew put up her right hand. "There's no point in confrontation with the nincompoop. What I do, and you should too, is go straight to our key contact there. His name is Bruce Peters, and he will bend over backward to help us out. I'll give you his private cell number.

"Not only is Bruce an excellent investigator, always up-to-date on the latest science, but he knows the lay of the land up here. When I say that, I mean he knows who can be trusted."

Judith nodded. "I see. I'll check with him first."

"Yes, and use my name. We have a deal, Bruce and I—he takes care of what I need from the crime lab, and I coach his casting."

"His *casting*?"

"He's trying to improve his fly-fishing technique."

Judith shook her head as she walked toward the door. "I know I'll figure this out eventually."

"One more thing you should know," said Lew, stopping her. "Doc Osborne is my best friend. No, actually, he's more than that."

"A significant other?"

"That's one way to put it," said Lew with a slight smile. "And he usually stops by for a final cup of coffee after his morning chat with his buddies at McDonald's. So don't be surprised if—"

"If I find a forensic odontologist emptying your coffeepot?"

* * *

An hour later there was a knock on Lew's door. Judith poked her head in. "I just got that autopsy report in from the Wausau Crime Lab," she said. "I think you'll want to see it right away, so I forwarded it.

Lew brought the autopsy report up on her computer screen while Judith sat down in one of the chairs in front of Lew's desk. She waited quietly while Lew studied the report. A minute later, she listened in silence as Lew picked up her phone and placed a call to the lawyer for the Knudsen family.

Lew pursed her lips before saying, "Martha, Chief Stern has made a big mistake. Just want you to know." And she ended the call.

"Is that true?" asked Judith. "Chief Stern was not aware that the girl didn't drown?"

"Maybe he chose *not* to know, but the crime lab's autopsy states she died of blunt-force trauma to her head and neck. No water in her lungs."

"I can't believe he didn't know there was a witness who might have helped with the investigation." Judith sounded appalled. "Wouldn't that person have been standing right there?"

"The lawyer for the family told me the witness was a weekend visitor who—from a distance and possibly hidden by brush along the shoreline—saw the couple fighting, but she didn't report seeing the fight because she saw a patrol car arrive at the scene and assumed the police were already involved. It wasn't until this weekend that the individual learned from the family that their daughter's death had been ruled accidental, so she came forward."

"So the only report was one stating it had been an accident?"

"Correct. Stern did not send a report to the crime lab. Instead he accepted the coroner's certification that it was an accidental death by drowning with no questions raised. That report he registered with the county only – not the Wausau Crime Lab. Hard to believe but that is exactly what Chief Stern did."

Lew tapped the end of her pen on the desk, thinking. When she raised her eyes to Judith's, she said, "Alan Stern appears to have neglected to question the circumstances surrounding the girl's drowning—for some reason. And that reason better be good. Very good. It's obvious he did not know there was a witness. In the meantime, Judith, thank you. Good work."

"All I did was call one of your Wausau boys."

"As soon as you were asked to do so. I appreciate that."

Judith got up and walked toward the door, then stopped and turned, asking, "Does the Wausau Crime Lab keep files on some of the accidental deaths up here? Even ones from years ago?"

"Only those accidents in which questions may have been raised regarding extenuating circumtances. Those accident case files are definitely kept. A long-standing practice and one that continues," said Lew. "Not all are available online, however. As I mentioned to you earlier, they have been working, as we have here at the county and our three police departments, to digitize paper files from years ago. Not sure how far they've gotten on that."

"I see," said Judith, and she left the room.

*   *   *

It was eight thirty when Osborne dropped by for his coffee. He wasn't alone. A tall, fair-haired man with a good tan and wearing white tennis shorts and a light-blue short-sleeved T-shirt followed him in. Lew guessed him to be in his midthirties.

"Good morning, Sheriff Ferris," said Doc, signaling with the use of her title that this wasn't a casual visit, "I don't know if you've ever met Herm's son-in-law, Bob Henman."

"I have not," said Lew, extending her hand. "Have a seat, you two. What can I help you with?"

"This won't take long," said Osborne, "but Bob runs a tennis program for high school students during the summer months, and he recently had an experience with the young Brinkerhoff boy that I think you should hear about."

Bob squirmed in the chair, looking uncomfortable as he said, "Maybe I should be careful here. I don't want to say anything that I could be sued for."

"Don't worry. Whatever you say is off the record," said Lew. "So you teach Barry Brinkerhoff?"

"I *did* teach the kid. I asked his father not to bring him again. Not after his behavior on the courts."

"Something negative, from the sound of it," said Lew.

"Alarming is more like it. He was in a mixed doubles match that he and his partner were losing to two girls. I watched him getting angry with himself, so flustered he started double-faulting. When he and his partner lost a game and were switching sides with the other players, he took his racket and smacked one of the girls right across the face. Hard.

"I had to stop the match, get the girl some ice, and call her parents. It wasn't just a swipe—she was hurt. I encouraged her parents to take her to the emergency room; I was afraid she might lose an eye."

"Is she okay?"

"Yes, thank goodness. This happened a couple weeks ago. Right before I heard about the Jet Ski accident and poor Sharon Knudsen.

"Sheriff Ferris, someone in a position of authority needs to talk to that boy—and his father."

"His father?"

"Yes. I called Mr. Brinkerhoff to let him know about the incident. He blew me off. Told me to mind my own business. That's not all. The father, Matt, plays doubles with a couple guys I know. Not often but when he's up here staying at their summer place. Seems he's smashed a couple tennis rackets while playing with those guys. That's pretty unusual for a casual tennis player."

"So you're saying anger issues might be a family tradition?"

"I hadn't thought of it quite that way. I was thinking the old man sets a pretty bad example. Not surprising, I guess, given what he's done in the past."

"Sounds like you know the family well." Lew sat forward in her chair. This was getting interesting.

"My grandfather was an assistant tennis coach at a college down in eastern Indiana. He took a summer job teaching tennis at Camp Ashwabagon, which is how our family ended up living here in the Northwoods. Barry Brinkerhoff's father was a young camper in those days. My grandfather may be nearing ninety, but he remembers those days. When I mentioned the incident with Barry, he said young Matt had been a handful too."

"Did he say more?"

"No, but I got the impression he might have bullied some of the other kids at camp. There's always one. Never fails. I got the same issue with some of the kids in my program—boys and girls both."

Lew looked over at Osborne. "This is good to know. Bob, don't worry. What you've told me will remain confidential, but it certainly helps in light of other observations people have made. Thank you for coming in."

The two men left, and Lew pulled her to-do lists up on her computer screen. Until now she'd had only the one position to fill ASAP: chief of the Loon Lake Police Department. But now she was adding another: chief of the Deer Haven Police.

Chapter Thirteen

It was midmorning Friday when Deer Haven chief of police Alan Stern, shoulders hunched and hands thrust deep into his pants pockets, ambled across the room to take a chair in front of Lew's desk. The expression on his face reminded her of a weasel: the nostrils twisted to one side as if sniffing something nasty, the eyes too close, the head itself too long and narrow.

Lew made a mental note to ask Osborne what caused some people to have such odd-shaped skulls. She remembered a conversation in which he'd said that in his late teens he had enjoyed sketching people's heads and modeling the skulls in clay during his art class.

After that experience, he had decided to become a sculptor, but that was before his father had made his feelings clear, telling him, "Forget it, Paul. That is one hard way to make a living," adding that he would not pay for college if Osborne didn't change his mind.

Oddly, Osborne had been surprised to find similar satisfaction in dentistry as he worked with images of skulls, cheekbones, jaws, and teeth. The result had been not just satisfaction with his work as a dentist but pleasure in studying the ever-changing science of odontology, which continued to mesh with new discoveries in DNA research.

*   *   *

Stern spoke first, with his usual disdainful tone. "Judge Voelker agreed with me and Coroner Pecore that the victim drowned after she landed headfirst on the same submerged log that the personal watercraft had hit and was knocked unconscious," he said. "Sheriff Ferris, you are in no position to question the judge and the coroner."

"What are you talking about?" asked Lew, deciding to see how far he would go with his lies. "I checked with Judge Perriman's office, and they haven't seen the final accident report. And what does Judge Voelker have to do with this case?"

"It's been filed with Judge Voelker in Carter County." Stern looked so self-satisfied that Lew want to punch him.

"Wait a minute," she said, shaking her right index finger at Stern. "You have no right to take this case to Carter County. How did that happen?"

Uncertainty glimmered in Stern's eyes. No doubt he'd wheedled an excuse from an inexperienced young clerk in the office of the McBride County Court that had allowed him to move the case to Voelker's domain. She suspected why, too.

A small, bald man in his fifties, Voelker was known to be a little too eager to satisfy the wealthy donors who backed his election campaigns. It was well known among the lawyers trying cases before him that he had barely managed to pass the Wisconsin bar.

That might explain why he went out of his way to annoy the women lawyers forced to deal with him by making asides that tipped too close to sexual innuendo. Among Lew's colleagues in law enforcement and legal circles, he was commonly referred to as "The Carter County Creep."

"You can't do anything about this case," said Stern, getting to his feet with a belligerent look on his face. "It'll be decided in Carter County." He headed for the door.

"Sit down," said Lew, her voice calm as she set the copy of the autopsy report down on her desk. Leaning forward on her elbows, she said, "There is no accident report. I have an official autopsy report from the Wausau Crime Lab stating the victim died of blunt-force trauma."

"Wh-a-a-t?" he stuttered, then threw his hands in the air. "You are out of your league, lady."

"Further," said Lew, "there is a witness willing to testify there was no Jet Ski accident and that she observed

Barry Brinkhoff assaulting Sharon Knudsen on the beach. She has a video that shows the assault taking place and that will be admissible in court.

"Chief Stern, I am requesting a warrant for the arrest of Barry Brinkerhoff."

Stern stared at her, his mouth slack.

"And yes, Alan Stern, you are fired. You are expected in the office next door to mine, where you will meet with my senior administrator, Dani Wright, who will relieve you of your badge, your nine-millimeter weapon, and your department communication devices. You may not leave the building until I've received notice from Ms. Wright that the proper procedures have been followed."

She stood up. "Alan Stern, you are free to leave."

"You are violating law enforcement standards," said Stern, his voice squeaking. "I'll see you in court." He waved an angry index finger as he got to his feet.

Saying nothing, Lew waited.

Stern crossed the room and yanked the door shut behind him. Lew shrugged. She was sheriff of McBride County. *Game on.*

After a few minutes of thought, she picked up the phone and called Martha Burns, the Knudsen family's lawyer.

"Stern's right about one thing," said Martha. "The case has been moved to Carter County, all right. Seems the victim's father was a fraternity brother of our McBride County's Judge Perriman."

"Oh, I see," said Lew.

"What you will find interesting, Sheriff Ferris, is that there's been no hearing scheduled, no charges filed—even though I am confident Voelker has received the original accident report. If you want my opinion," said the lawyer, "if the case stays in Carter County, there won't be any hearing. Voelker and the Brinkerhoff kid's old man will just keep stalling until the case is forgotten."

"Can they do that?"

The lawyer chuckled. "No. What they don't know yet is that we have the witness I told you about, the woman on a paddleboard who saw the entire encounter."

"Anything else I should know?"

"Your Chief Stern's father has been the caretaker for the Brinkerhoff family's property for thirty years."

"Ah," said Lew, "well, I am about to request a warrant for the arrest of Barry Brinkerhoff. Will I have to go through Carter County and Voelker?"

"No," said Martha, "the assault occurred here, so Judge Perriman can issue the warrant. The case may be heard elsewhere, and I am sure it will be moved from Carter County."

"That's all I need to know," said Lew. "Thank you."

Her next call was to the office of McBride County Judge Richard Perriman.

*　　*　　*

A commotion in the corridor outside her office caused Lew to look up just as a six-foot, four-inch figure barged into the room. Wearing khaki fishing shorts and a T-shirt emblazoned *Fishing with Ray: Excitement, Romance and Live Bait*, the unexpected visitor was as familiar as the contents of the Ziploc bag he held in one hand: bluegills. Fresh-caught and perfectly cleaned bluegills, the tastiest fish in the Northwoods.

"Hey, Sheriff Ferris, tried dropping these by Doc's place, but no one was home," said Ray. "I don't want them sitting outdoors, so do you mind?" Before she could answer, he had walked over to the small fridge under the coffeemaker and slipped the Ziploc inside.

"Heavens no, thank you," said Lew with a grin of surprise. The morning was perking up.

"You are as welcome as the flowers," said Ray, dark eyes twinkling over the easy smile.

Before Lew could say more, Dani walked into the office, a hesitant look on her face as she said, "Mr. Pradt, could I ask you a favor?"

Ray turned his face to her and smiled. "Sure, but you gotta drop the *mister*." Again the twinkle and the smile. Lew watched Dani melt and couldn't blame her.

Ray Pradt had opted out of a traditional life years earlier. While his two siblings went on to stellar careers in their fields—his brother following their father into medicine to become a hand surgeon and his sister establishing herself as a well-regarded litigator with a Chicago law firm—Ray chose to follow his passion over the lakes and rivers and into the forests of the Northwoods.

He liked to brag that his family of origin had evolved from the roots of old-growth hemlock, or maybe it was the balsam and birch. Whatever. Red pine, Norway pine, white pine: he claimed all were kin.

When other kids went to Boy Scout camp, Ray camped out with an elderly Ojibwa fishing guide who taught him how to read the water for big fish, whether muskie, walleye, or bass. The old man knew the woods, too, and from him Ray learned the meaning of a turned leaf or a crushed pinecone and the sign of a lone wolf—or a pack.

When it came time for college, Ray persuaded his parents to allow him to take a year off and work for a local bait shop owner. He soon learned everything there was to know about minnows, crayfish, wrigglers, night crawlers, crickets, wax worms, even leeches. During that summer he also apprenticed as a fishing guide. He never went off to school. Though his dad was furious, Ray insisted on going his own way, convincing his parents he could support himself.

He didn't mention that one week he had to sleep in an abandoned bear den, but that didn't last long. He soon found part-time work helping to dig graves at St. Mary's Cemetery. That work paid off unexpectedly, as he found that one of the discarded, inexpensive caskets could double as a place to store fresh-caught leeches until they could be sold.

No one could accuse Ray Pradt of lack of entrepreneurial instinct. Making money might not be his forte, but having fun? Few could outdo him when it came to appreciation, sheer enjoyment, of the outdoors.

But all was not ideal. In his late teens he started drinking. At first it seemed a refreshing way to cap a long day on the water: reminisce about "the one that got away" with the guys at the bar, have one more beer rather than head back to his small trailer, have yet another beer or three or a slug of Jack Daniel's before dropping off to sleep.

The night he thought he had run over a person only to find it was a deer was the night he forced himself to be honest. The next morning he canceled a guiding trip and called a buddy he knew was in AA.

He changed his life—and surprise, after quitting drinking, he caught more fish. Cleaning up his act meant longer days on the water. It also meant setting out early in the morning with a sense of freshness, a fresh feeling that had disappeared when he was sodden with alcohol.

He became legendary in the region for his ability to track predatory wolves and the elusive cougar, to find lost hunters and family dogs. He was also remarkably skilled at finding private water, the small private lakes that held marvelous large walleye. More than once he had barely eluded the game wardens who knew of his proclivity for the illegal catch.

His talents did not go unnoticed. More than once during their morning coffees at McDonald's, one of Osborne's retired buddies, while updating the crew on Ray's latest catch—or misdemeanor—would invariably end with the comment, "Doncha know that razzbonya can track a snake over a rock?"

And even though Ray's habit of smoking weed in a state where it was not yet legal had led to a modest misdemeanor file in Lew's office, that proved to be yet another talent, as he brought his ability to adapt to nature, and to the "natures" around him, in a way that proved invaluable to her surveillance of bad actors. He knew who lived in what remote location. People could hide from the law, even the IRS, but they couldn't hide from Ray Pradt.

* * *

Right now, however, it seemed it was Ray who couldn't hide from Dani Wright. Not that Lew knew if that would be his intention or not.

Before Dani could ask her question, Lew interrupted with, "Ray, do you happen to know the Brinkerhoffs? They have a place over on Hemlock Lake."

"Of course I know the Brinkerhoffs," said Ray, his voice mocking the gruff tones of his ex-client. "Doesn't everyone? Velly important people, doncha know."

"I'm serious," said Lew, in no mood for goofiness.

"Sorry," said Ray with a wink at Dani. "Be with you in a second, hon," he told her. "Yes, Sheriff Ferris, I know the family. I guided the old man, Matt, and his son over on Big Muskellunge Lake maybe two, three years ago. Took 'em out twice, but no luck.

"Problem was Matt. The guy won't take direction. I recommended a surface bait, and he refused to give up his damn Suick. Said it always worked for him. Well, goddammit, if that was the case, then why was he paying me a hundred bucks an hour?

"Anyway, the kid couldn't have been less interested in fishing. He played video games on his phone while the geezer sitting off in the corner of the pontoon made his way through a six-pack, and all this was before ten o'clock in the morning."

"Who's the geezer? The grandfather?"

"No, you know, old Judge Voelker. He's been around forever."

"So Judge Voelker was fishing with you?"

Ray leveled his eyes at Lew. "I don't call inhaling six-packs of Leinenkugel fishing."

"Thank you," said Lew. "So it was Matt Brinkerhoff who hired you and not his father. Right?"

"Yes. But that was two years ago. I haven't run into that bunch since, though I see they've built quite the place out on that point on Hemlock Lake. Too bad they tore down the old lodge, though—beautiful building, y'know, historic."

Lew turned to her senior admin. "Sorry to interrupt, Dani. He's all yours. Good luck." Then she busied herself at her desk, still curious to see what was up with Dani.

Chapter Fourteen

"My best friend is visiting from Madison late this afternoon, and she wants to learn to fish," said Dani, sounding so breathless Lew had to wonder if it was a lie. "Me too. I want to learn."

The look of surprise on Ray's face said it all: why on earth would a young woman as dedicated to her physical appearance as Dani be interested in getting close to a slimy fish? A dirt-laden night crawler? Something was wrong with this picture.

"Oh," said Ray, making an obvious attempt to be sporting. "Gee, Dani, this isn't the best time to fish. In August the water is so warm the fish slow down, and they stay very deep in the lake."

The disappointment in Dani's eyes stopped him, and the thirty-two-year-old guide backed off his professional approach to reconsider. "Well, if it's learning how to cast a spinning rod and all about bait and tackle, I guess we could do it."

Lew could hear the reluctance in his voice, and she didn't blame him. Dani Wright going fishing seemed like an oxymoron. Then it dawned on Lew. Dani's interest in Ray had nothing to do with fish. She should have remembered—Dani was interested in Ray.

And Ray Pradt was nothing if not an attractive young man, which explained the number of women sidling up to introduce themselves or swiping right in his direction on Bumble, the dating app. It wasn't that Ray preyed on women; it was quite the opposite. He was also kind, which was becoming more obvious by the moment as he tried to let Dani down easy.

"Fishing is something I have really wanted to learn," she said, trying to sound convincing.

Maybe, but not likely. Lew knew Dani had recently been through the breakup of a long-term relationship with a young man named Wayne, who was the exact opposite of Ray.

Wayne, heavy shouldered with a scruffy black beard, was a type often found in the Northwoods. He put every dime he owned into a spanking new pickup with "pipes" that roared when he accelerated. Going down the road, he played music on his truck speakers so loud that nearby drivers could feel the pounding in their own cars even with the windows up.

And it was no secret that Wayne's sketchy résumé, most recently as a pizza delivery man, would not be enough to support a young family, much less pay for Dani's hair, eyebrow, and nail regimens. While she was making good money in her work for the McBride County Sheriff's Department, Lew suspected Dani was a traditionalist at heart. She hoped for a man to love and support her. The clue was in the bridal sites she checked each morning after sitting down at her computer.

*   *   *

Lew repressed a smile as she observed the impossible position Ray was in. He knew how valuable Dani's IT work was for Lew, especially with the added responsibilities of the sheriff's department. As critical as his work could be to Lew's pursuit of lost tourists or miscreants breaking the law, Dani's aptitude for staying abreast of the latest advances in technology, ranging from smartphones to data searches, made her as valuable an asset to Lew as he was.

"Okay, okay." Ray raised his hands and struggled to smile as he relented, saying, "Meet me for breakfast at my place tomorrow morning, and I'll take you ladies out on my pontoon. Write down my address, and let me know if you need directions—"

"No, I don't," said Dani. "I got your number on my phone. I can track you easy."

A look of alarm crossed Ray's face. Lew could imagine what he was thinking. *Track him?* Track him where? But he didn't say anything.

"Thank you so much, Ray," said Dani. "And please, Cindy and I are happy to pay you whatever."

Judith had walked in during the conversation and caught Lew's eye with a wry smile.

"You have a question?" Lew asked Judith.

"I do," said Judith.

After giving her a quick introduction to Ray, Lew motioned for her to follow her back to Dani's office. As they left the room, she could hear Ray instructing his new student on what to wear. More important, Lew could hear him telling her what *not* to wear.

"You'll be climbing on and off my pontoon, and we may wade some too. Might be muddy. Got something sturdy for your feet? A hat that won't blow off? Something with long sleeves in case the sun is out. And this is real important: the kind of sunscreen that doesn't kill fish . . ."

*   *   *

Walking into Dani's office, where Judith's desk and computer had been set up, Lew said to Judith, "You haven't met Ray Pradt before, have you?"

"No, but I remember years ago that his father was a resident training under my father at St. Mary's Hospital. Dad liked him. I imagine his son is a pretty good guy?"

"A little too good in the looks department," said Lew with a chuckle. "I have to say, it's remarkable how many

women fall all over the razzbonya. I wonder if they realize that if they actually ended up hooked to Mr. Pradt—
and pardon my fishing metaphor—they'd be supporting
him for the rest of their life. Guiding fishermen is not a
lucrative career path."

"I'm sure you're right," said Judith, "but on the other
hand, he appears to be a very happy man, and that's
worth money. Right?" She smiled. "Speaking of fishing,
I was going to ask you when you're likely to offer your
next class in fly-fishing. One of the sales clerks at Ralph's
Sporting Goods told me you teach sometimes."

"I used to," said Lew. "That was before I was elected
sheriff. Right now I barely have time for myself to fish,
even to grab lunch, much less teach a class." She paused,
then said, "Oh, heck, what are you doing tomorrow? It's
the weekend, I need a day off, and the weather is promising. If you're up for an early start, you're welcome to
come along."

"That would be wonderful, but are you sure?"

"Judith, I need a break, and time in the water is the
best therapy money can't buy."

"But I'll pay you for lessons."

"Not tomorrow. We'll see how you do first."

"Deal," said Judith, extending her hand.

"Deal." Walking back to her office, Lew felt good.
She liked the woman. This fishing outing would be a
good time to get to know her better.

Chapter Fifteen

As Lew walked into her now empty office, her phone rang. It was Judge Perriman's office. Now Lew had what she'd been waiting for since firing Alan Stern early that morning: the warrant for the arrest of Barry Brinkerhoff.

With a quick call on her personal cell, she reached Officer Todd Donovan, her longtime right-hand colleague from the Loon Lake Police Department, and arranged for him to accompany her as backup.

"Shouldn't take long, Todd," she said, after reaching him in his squad car.

"I'll be there in less than ten minutes, Chief—I mean Sheriff," said Todd, quickly correcting himself.

"Quiet in town? Did you get your application in to apply for my old spot?" she asked him as he climbed into her cruiser. She was still getting used to the car, a brand-new model for the brand-new sheriff.

"I did," said the young officer. "Turned it in yesterday to the mayor's office. They said the city council may meet as early as next week, but there are two other candidates. At least that's what I hear."

It was a good twenty-five minutes to Hemlock Lake. The cruiser pulled up to iron gates, and Lew put down her window to announce their arrival. She identified herself and waited a couple of minutes, and finally the gates swung open.

"This is a long driveway," she commented as they neared the sprawling glass house tucked under a canopy of pine trees. "Quite the place, huh?" It was a rhetorical question. She pulled into a parking spot alongside a black Range Rover.

"Thirty million dollars," said Todd. "I know because my brother-in-law was a subcontractor on the place. The guy he worked for is getting sued for over a million by the owners."

"Really?" Lew gave Todd a questioning look as she opened the door. "What's the problem?"

"The usual," said Todd as they started up the stone walkway to the massive doors marking the entrance the house. He lowered his voice. "The owners used a California architect who insisted on using certain suppliers. The lawsuit alleges shoddy materials." Todd grinned. "Apparently there's a wing with bedrooms, and they've discovered sound carries. Kind of embarrassing, I guess."

"Huh," said Lew as she reached for the ivory bird's egg marking the doorbell.

A man wearing the uniform of a security guard answered the door. "Come in, Sheriff Ferris. What can I do for you? Mr. Brinkerhoff is about to rush off to catch his plane, so I'll try to help you out."

"I have a warrant for the arrest of Barry Brinkerhoff—"

"Barry? What the hell—" Interrupting her, a tall, blond-haired man had appeared from behind the security guard. He pushed the security guard aside. "I'm Matthew Brinkerhoff, Barry's father. What's this all about?"

Ignoring him, Lew continued. ". . . for felony assault with intent to cause bodily harm and resulting in the death of a young woman by the name of Sharon Knudsen on the date of—"

"Barry, get out here," said the man in a loud voice.

A sullen-looking teenage boy came slouching from around the same corner. Lew noticed he had the pale, square face and light-blond hair of his father.

"Sign that paper so these people can leave. I got a plane to catch." He turned to the security guard and said, "Call my pilot and tell him I'll be a few minutes late."

"Nothing to sign," said Lew. "Barry Brinkerhoff, you're under arrest for felony assault with intent to cause bodily harm—"

"You said that," said the father, stepping toward Lew.

"You will be coming with us—"

"Oh, hold on there," said the father. "I'm calling my lawyer. He can handle this. My son isn't going anywhere."

"Your lawyer is welcome to handle this at the McBride County Court House," said Lew.

She stepped forward to put handcuffs on the teenager, only to have his father step in front of the boy. The expression in the man's eyes was the same one Lew had seen once too often in the eyes of her ex-husband: an expression that meant he was about to slug her. She had only had to see it once before filing for divorce.

"Careful, sir," said Todd in an even tone. "Please step back, or I'll have to arrest you for—"

"All right, I'm back," said the older man, his hands up. "Go with them, Barry. I'll meet you at the courthouse." He turned to the security guard. "Call my plane. Tell them to cancel the flight until they hear from me.'" He stomped off and disappeared around the corner, cursing as he went.

"Do you need a jacket?" Lew asked the boy before she and Todd turned to escort him down to the cruiser. The boy shook his head and said nothing. He remained silent during the rest of the ride to town, where they were met by a lawyer from the office of the district attorney.

The formal arraignment took place an hour later. Matthew Brinkerhoff did not show up, but his lawyer did. A criminal complaint was filed, and it was arranged for bail to be set the next morning. Barry Brinkerhoff was informed that he would spend the night in the McBride County Jail. If bail was posted before noon on the following day, he could be released.

As Barry was led off to jail, Lew got a call from Martha Burns, the Knudsen family lawyer. "Thank you, Sheriff Ferris," she said. "The family thanks you too. There is a long way to go, but this helps."

As Lew hung up, she shivered. Something had happened during that trip to the house on Hemlock Lake. The look in Matthew Brinkerhoff's eyes had triggered an uncomfortable response, one she had not had since her divorce: a feeling of terror.

Chapter Sixteen

Late that afternoon, after hearing from Osborne that he'd made a reservation at seven that evening for a fish fry at the Loon Lake Pub, Lew decided to pack up her files and finish the workday at her farm.

She looked forward to sitting down by her little lake (or as Osborne would kid whenever she mentioned her tiny hint of heaven, "It's a *pond*, Lewellyn—not a lake"). Yes, time for the farm, time for closing her eyes and letting the breezes wash away the nightmare she had seen in Brinkerhoff's eyes.

Walking by Dani's office on her way out, she heard Judith on the phone saying, "Mr. Peters, I can't thank you enough . . . oh, sure, Bruce. Look forward to meeting you in person one of these days, Bruce. And, again, thank you."

Oh, thought Lew, pausing to listen, *I wonder what it was that Bruce had to say?* More on the Knudsen case? She waited until she heard Judith end the call.

"Excuse me," said Lew, walking into the room, "but I heard you on the phone. Was that Bruce Peters from the Wausau Crime Lab? Is there an update on the Knudsen autopsy report? I was under the impression the medical examiner had submitted a final version."

Worry crossed Judith's face as she said, "Yes, that was Mr. Peters, but I had asked him to see if he could find the file on my sister's death, and we were talking about that. I hope that was okay. I realize it's a personal matter . . ."

"No, fine," said Lew. "I can't imagine anyone having an issue with that. Those are public records. Did he find it for you?"

"Yes." Judith paused, then said, "Do you mind if we don't discuss it right now?" She tightened her lips, and Lew could see the woman was on the verge of tears.

"Of course." Lew began to back out of the room. "These things can be upsetting even though a great deal of time may have passed."

She started to walk away, then stopped, turned back, and before she knew what she was doing, she said, "I lost my son ten years ago, and I feel that loss every day. That pain does not go away."

Surprise crossed Judith's face. "I'm sorry to hear that. Did he have cancer or . . . something?" Lew could hear Judith trying to focus on something other than her own sad news.

"It was a fight outside a bar where teenagers hung out. He was knifed by an older kid angry over a girl. Severed his carotid artery. No one called for an ambulance until it was too late." Lew was quiet, remembering. Shaking her head, she said, "Yeah, that was hard. I loved that kid . . . and Jamie was only sixteen. Too young."

"That's how old my sister was," said Judith. She pressed her hands against her eyes, covering them as she spoke. "She wasn't killed in a boating accident either. I knew that. I was only eight years old, but I knew that. My parents lied. They lied and lied and lied."

She held her breath for a moment before saying, "She was sexually assaulted and died of blunt trauma to her head. That's what I just learned. It's in the cold case files down at the crime lab. Why wasn't anyone honest?"

With those words, Judith dropped her head into her hands and wept. Lew walked over to put an arm across her shoulders.

"It's okay," said Lew. "Take it easy . . . that may have been the only way your parents could deal with it."

Judith wiped at her eyes and looked up at Lew. "The person who killed her was never charged. The file states that the police were never able to identify a suspect. You know, we forget that in those days, DNA science was not where it is today."

"You're right about that," said Lew. "That's why Doc Osborne and his father before him, as dentists, were the best sources for identifying dead bodies. In those days, teeth were the most reliable means of identification. Today, bones and teeth, even skin and body fluids, can provide searchable DNA samples. But not in those days."

"I know that my parents were relieved that they didn't have to go through an ugly trial that would have caused them to grieve even more."

"So your sister's death is in cold case files?"

Judith gave a weak smile. "Yes. There was something else in the file, too, which may explain my parents' response to the autopsy findings. Bruce Peters said there is a note in the file saying it had something to do with not trusting the coroner in those days." Judith wiped at her wet cheeks and reached for a Kleenex.

"He said the man was known to take naked photos of victims' bodies. Only women, of course, and show them around like they were some sort of porn or something. So people whose female relatives died weren't eager to have autopsies done or let the coroner near the body. Disgusting. But that fits with what I heard my parents say to the police officer who came to our house that morning. That's why my dad insisted that one of his colleagues be allowed to identify my sister's body and that only the Wausau Crime Lab could conduct the autopsy."

"I heard about that guy," said Lew. "Pecore isn't much better, but he's not that bad."

She leaned against the wall and waited. She wanted to be sure Judith was okay before she left. After a few minutes, when the woman appeared to have gathered herself together, Lew said, "I am so sorry about this. Are you sure you're going to be okay? Any old friends you can call?"

Judith's face changed: a grim determination settled over her features.

"I'm going to be fine. Now that I know what I always suspected . . . I'm going to be fine."

Maybe the harsh news gave her some kind of closure, thought Lew.

"Did the file have the name of the individual involved?"

"Yes and no. There were three boys involved. They were junior counselors at Camp Ashwabagon. Each boy accused the others and insisted he was innocent. Supposedly at the time there was no evidence to say one way or the other. Like we just said, there was no DNA in those days."

"So all you have is the connection to Camp Ashwabagon?"

"Yes. Bruce said the boys were juveniles, so their names were redacted. The answer is no, no names." Judith sighed, appearing to come to terms with the news. "At least I know they were counselors at that camp. That's more than I've known all these years. I'll have to be satisfied with that much." She wiped at her cheeks and tried to smile. "Thank you for listening."

"Happy to," said Lew. "If you feel you need to talk about it more, I'm here. Okay?"

Judith nodded.

Chapter Seventeen

People of all ages were packed into the Loon Lake Pub that evening. No surprise. It was the usual Friday night fish fry crowd with a noise level so high Lew had to shout to make herself heard. Leaning forward on his elbows, Osborne tried to hear what she was saying.

"I wish I could have said the right thing," said Lew in her loudest voice.

"Wh-a-a-t?" Osborne looked puzzled.

"When Judith told me what she learned about her sister's death. How she had been sexually assaulted and died of blunt-force trauma."

"Sexual assault? I never heard about that," said Osborne. "But I was a kid then. My dad wouldn't have shared that information even if he had known."

"The look on her face broke my heart. I couldn't help remembering my son's death."

Osborne reached for Lew's hand and held it as the table next to theirs, a party of twelve with a toddler having a screaming tantrum, got up to leave. He waited for things to quiet down before saying in a normal voice, "Lewellyn, we've both been there, haven't we? When my dad had to tell me that my mother was gone, I was only six years old, but I will never forget that moment: his face, my heart. And you with your son, Jamie. I know you wish you could change things, but what can you do? What can any of us do? Life can be hard."

"I'm glad I invited her to fish with us tomorrow. Maybe that'll help a bit."

"Fishing helped you."

*　　*　　*

Osborne's remark reminded Lew of the days after her son's death, days she'd spent in the trout stream with her fly rod and her grief. It had been months since she had split from her husband and demanded sole custody of their two children. Knowing she was overwhelmed with grief, her grandfather had taken her daughter, Suzanne, into his home during that time.

"I know what you need, Lewellyn. Go," her grandfather had said. The man who had taught her to fly-fish was wise in ways she didn't appreciate until years later.

And so, Lew, alone on the water, had waded and wept and wept and waded. It was twelve days before she walked back into her grandfather's house, set down her fly rod, and hugged her daughter. Two days later, after reading a feature story in the local newspaper highlighting the success of a new program recently launched at the nearby community college, Lew picked up the phone. She made an appointment to enroll in the Northwoods Community Technical College's Criminal Justice program, Law Enforcement Division.

It was time to tackle life on her terms.

* * *

"Is Judith a fly-fisherman?" asked Osborne, bringing Lew's attention back to their conversation.

"No," said Lew, "but she seems interested. We'll see. At the very least it should take her mind off things . . . maybe."

* * *

The late August morning held a hint of autumn in the cool breeze that was blowing the next morning when Lew and Osborne picked Judith up at her home and drove south in Lew's pickup. When they got to the clearing where Lew liked to park, she got out two pairs of waders, two rod cases, her old fly-fishing vest, a spinning rod, and a small booklet. Osborne unloaded his gear and pulled on his waders.

"Hey, Doc, good luck," said Lew, watching as Osborne waded into the water and set off upstream to practice his casting.

"Careful, Judith. Do not watch me," said Osborne, moving slowly through the riffles. "I'm the worst at double hauling you'll ever see." He gave a wave and a laugh as he disappeared behind a nearby bend in the river.

"What's a double haul?" asked Judith.

"Don't ask until you have to," said Osborne, calling back over his shoulder.

With Osborne on his way, Lew turned to Judith. "Okay, we're going to start with some basics. Then, if you find you're interested in this sport, I'll suggest a better teacher than me."

"Based on what I've heard, that's not true," said Judith.

"We'll see. Let's start with these waders," said Lew. "You appear to be about the same size as my daughter, Suzanne, so I'll have you try on her waders and boots."

"These are new to me," said Judith as she stepped into the waders. Both women were relieved when Suzanne's boots fit just fine.

"Next item," said Lew, handing her student a fly-fishing vest. "This is one of my old ones. If you decide to get into this sport, you'll want to try on a few until you feel the perfect fit." She continued with mock seriousness. "Judith, meet your new best friend. Your fly-fishing vest will carry everything you need in the trout stream: your trout flies, all the equipment you will need for changing flies or adding line, your cell phone in a waterproof case, any snacks you may want when you take a break, a full bottle of water, and, given you and I are ladies, some toilet tissue."

"All that in this?" Judith sounded amazed.

"Yep. And it shouldn't be too heavy in case you fall in." With those words, Lew grinned. "I'm kidding."

* * *

In the hour of instruction that followed while Lew and Judith waded in the stream, Lew described the difference between a spinning rod and a fly rod, demonstrating each as she talked. Then the differences between bait fishing and fly-fishing, and why trout fishermen practiced catch-and-release while bait fishermen were able to keep and eat their bluegills, walleyes, bass, and muskie. "If they want," said Lew, "that's legal, though many bait fishermen also prefer to catch and release. There is a reason why we trout fishermen practice catch-and-release."

She continued. "Brook trout, which are native to our region, can be—and have been—overfished over the years. Catch-and-release saves the fish and gives the fly-fisherman another day to find peace in the river. This is true for rainbow trout too.

"But here's a key difference between the two kinds of fishing: when you're bait fishing, you're *on* the water; when fly-fishing, you're *in* the water. Those are two quite different experiences.

"One keeps you safe in a boat or on a dock, while the other . . . let me just say that fly-fishing up a stream can take you into beautiful territory or into an area belonging to strangers who may not be up for visitors."

"Really?" asked Judith, her eyes widening. "But you're not trespassing when you're in the trout stream, are you?"

"Not unless you decide to climb out of the water. That's when you are on private land. And that's when you want to be sure the folks who live there don't eat their young."

Judith stared at her. "You're kidding, right?"

"Kind of," said Lew with a big smile, happy with her little joke. "Seriously, you do need to know where you are and who owns the land along that river or stream. Could be public, but it could be private. You need to be aware.

"Also, up here in the Northwoods it is easy to lose cell service, so safety can be an issue, especially if bad weather moves in. Believe me, that can happen when you're in a boat too. But when you're standing in a trout stream at a certain time of day, especially dusk, life can get interesting.

"It has happened to me more. Just two years ago I was up north fishing the Elroy River in Michigan when I discovered I had waded a little too close to a mother bear with her cubs. That can happen easier than you think."

"Dangerous sport, huh?"

"But worth it. Let me rephrase something I said a few minutes ago. When you're fly-fishing, you aren't just in the water: *you are one with the water.*"

The expression on Judith's face told Lew the woman was up for the challenge.

* * *

After an hour, they climbed up on shore and sat down to enjoy the picnic lunch Lew had packed: liverwurst sandwiches on rye with mustard, followed by molasses cookies. Lew set one sandwich and two cookies aside for Osborne.

"So, Lew," said Judith, "mind if I ask you how you got into law enforcement? I know it's been a relatively new career path for women."

"I don't mind. I sometimes wonder myself, since it's been a lucky choice for me."

Lew took a bite from her sandwich, then said, "I married way too young: the cute guy in high school, the cute guy who turned into the not-so-cute drunk. We had two kids right away, and when it became clear to me that the cute guy wasn't the type to hold a steady job, I landed a position as a secretary at the paper mill in Rhinelander. I hated it, but it was steady income.

"I got divorced when my kids were in middle school, which was okay for a while, but after my son's death, I knew I had to make a change. I had to do something where I could use my head, where I could do something to help people. I had been thinking about going back to school for a degree in social work, something like that—except for one drawback, which had to do with my childhood. I was raised, like a young wolf, outdoors."

Judith's eyebrows shot up.

"I knew you'd react that way," said Lew, chuckling. "Let me explain. I was raised by my widowed grandfather, my mother's father, who ran a small sporting goods store and bait shop. After our parents were killed in a car accident, he raised my brother and me. So I had grew up doing what Grandpa did: fish. My brother, too; we all three fished all the time, summer and winter, and had a great time.

"So when I had decided to change jobs, all I knew for sure was that whatever I did would have to be something I could do outdoors. So even as I considered social work, I also debated becoming a forest ranger, maybe a game warden. I wasn't sure.

"Not long after Jamie's death, I borrowed money from my grandfather and enrolled in the law enforcement program at the community college. One day the Loon Lake Police Department put up a notice at the school asking students to apply for a paid internship. That sounded interesting.

"I applied. I got the internship and when I finished the program at the college, Chief John Sloan offered me a job. That was almost twenty years ago, and I've been there ever since. I love it."

Lew finished her sandwich and nibbled at the cookie. "It hasn't been easy, but it sure as hell hadn't been boring." She grinned at Judith.

"And you're outdoors," said Judith.

"I was outdoors until I got elected sheriff. Now I worry that I'll be so busy that I'll have to fight to get outside. But I will."

The two women sat quietly finishing their cookies. "The job has saved my life," said Lew. "It got me through my years of grief."

"You're lucky," said Judith. "Not sure I'll ever get past mine."

Lew said nothing.

Chapter Eighteen

After they had finished, Lew sat down on a rock beside her student and, reaching into her gear bag, pulled out a booklet she had brought along. "When I suggest a better teacher than myself, what I mean is if you're serious about learning how to fly-fish, you may want to do what I did and go out to upstate New York to the Wulff School of Fly Fishing. It was started by Joan Wulff, who is an icon in the world of fly-fishing. She was my mentor," said Lew with a smile, remembering how much she had enjoyed the experience.

"Over a long weekend, you get introduced to everything from the science of the water and the fish to the basics of rods, trout flies, and casting.

"Meantime," she said as she held up the booklet, which was titled *Macroinvertebrate Life in the River*, "you may want to browse through this so you know what you're getting yourself into. Learning to use the right trout fly takes you into a whole new world."

She flipped through a couple of pages in the booklet, holding them out as she went. "Here we have the caddis fly larva, the dragonfly larva—my favorite, the midge larva, and the whirligig beetle. And that's for a start.

"You need to learn how to match your trout fly to the insect that the trout are feeding on. For example, what we call 'wet flies' match the insect life *under* the water, while 'dry flies' mimic insects in the air *over* the water."

She handed the booklet to Judith and watched as she flipped through a few pages before pausing to study one.

"Oh my God, a rat-tailed maggot larva? What on earth?"

"Welcome to fly-fishing," said Lew with a grin. "My favorites are dry flies." She pointed to several pinned to her fly-fishing vest. "I find them lovely to look at, and fish love 'em too.

"But that's your next lesson." She dropped her voice into a mock serious tone as she said, "If you choose to continue." Then Lew lightened up. "Judith, fly-fishing involves taking in a lot of information and spending a lot of time with a fly rod, so give it some thought before you decide if it's the sport for you."

"I certainly have the time," Judith said, before she was interrupted by the sound of someone moving through the water.

"Hey," said Osborne as he waded around the bend.

"Hurry up, Doc, before I finish your sandwich." Lew stood up and stretched as she waited for Osborne to join them.

*   *   *

"Judith, I shared the news about your sister with Doc," said Lew after they had finished their cookies. "He's experienced in forensic dentistry and helps me out as our acting coroner when our appointed numnut is too drunk to function."

"I hope you don't mind," said Osborne, watching Judith as he spoke, "but I think I'm just a year younger than you, and even though I didn't go to school in Loon Lake, I remember your family. My father was a dentist, too, and sometimes worked with your dad when he had patients needing dental surgery at the hospital."

"No, I don't mind," said Judith. "I plan to stay in touch with Bruce Peters at the Wausau Crime Lab, as he said he might have more information about my sister's death in their files. You work with those Wausau boys, don't you?" she asked with a slight smile, proving she knew the department lingo for their colleagues at the crime lab.

"I do," said Osborne, "but more important, I have a suggestion that may help your search."

Seeing the look of interest on Judith's face, Lew gave Osborne a nod of encouragement.

"It was in the late seventies when I joined my dad's dental practice and the Wisconsin Dental Association after graduating from Marquette University Dental School," said Osborne. "I had already developed a strong interest in dental forensics."

He paused and gave a grim smile. "We needed that up here, as the mobsters out of Chicago had a bad habit of hiding corpses in the woods. That was back in the thirties and forties, but we were finding them still. Even as late as the 1970s, teeth were the gold standard for identifying victims, but that was changing with the discovery of DNA.

"Through the dental association, I became familiar with a nationally prominent forensic pathologist, Dr. Thomas Kessinger, one of the pioneers in the field of forensics and the new science of DNA. He stressed the importance of finding ways to save dental records, blood samples, and samples of other bodily fluids collected whenever there was a death under unknown circumstances.

"Later, I studied with a forensic pathologist from the Wausau Crime Lab, Dr. Roger Nystrom, who was very keen on Kessinger's work and on the developments in the DNA science. In fact, he went east one year to study with Dr. Kessinger and returned anticipating the advances in DNA research that would explode in the eighties.

"Following Kessinger's advice, he would make microscopic slides of forensic evidence collected during rape examinations at regional hospitals and put those slides, marked with names and dates, into storage.

"Dr. Nystrom has since passed away, but I know the kinds of records he kept, and I may be able to help Bruce Peters find them. I have to believe that the crime lab did not destroy his evidence files. Lewellyn told me you've seen the report on your sister's death, but did you notice if there was an autopsy?"

"No, and I should have," said Judith. Lew could see that a change had come over her. Listening intently, she had inched closer to Osborne. "I didn't think to look or ask about that yesterday."

"Do I have your permission to call Bruce about this?" asked Osborne. "I will check my files too, as I'm sure my father's files, which I took over when he retired, may have your family's records. They may not be of any help, but who knows."

"Yes, please. But Dr. Osborne, are you saying that there may be more detailed records at the crime lab? Blood samples? Semen, maybe?"

"Not sure, but we can find out. If we do find that there are microscopic slides from your sister's autopsy, it may cost quite a bit of money to ask a lab to try to reconstitute the slides."

"I have a budget for cold case investigative work," said Lew, interrupting. "One of the advantages of running the sheriff's department. We should be able to cover that expense."

"And I have money, Dr. Osborne," said Judith. "I can pay for the research." Tears were visible on her cheeks. "Thank you both," she said. "If we find there is a semen sample, then I can learn who . . ."

"No promises," said Osborne. "Your sister was assaulted in the late sixties. The question is whether or not we can locate Dr. Nystrom's files. By the way, Judith"— Osborne smiled—"my friends call me Doc—just Doc."

"Oh golly, I'm going to owe Bruce another casting lesson," said Lew. She answered the question in Judith's eyes with, "Remember? I told you that's how I pay him back when he helps me on cases.

"Bruce makes sure I don't have to deal with his boss, the jerk who never hesitates to let me know women should not be in law enforcement. I have his personal cell number so I can reach him easily."

"I have a hunch he'll like helping us out with this," said Osborne. "Who knows, Lewellyn, if we get good news on the old files, your cold case work may change significantly."

Chapter Nineteen

In Chicago, Mallory was about to leave her apartment for a Saturday afternoon run along Lake Shore Drive when a late text message arrived on her cell phone. She studied it, checked her calendar, and decided to call Sarah.

"Hello, this is the Hatch Gallery, Sarah speaking."

"Hey, Sarah, you were supposed to give me a heads-up next time you're at the Brinkerhoffs'. I just got a notice there's a client event Monday night and you'll be there. What's up?"

"I am so sorry, Mal," said Sarah, "but I just found out myself. I wasn't planning to go until after Labor Day, but Matt's insisting, so, you know, I'll be there."

Mallory could hear her frustration over the phone.

"Afraid I'll have to show up too," said Mallory, "You know how the world works; I can't disappoint a million-dollar client. Looks like we're both in the same boat, dammit." She sighed. "I did have other meetings planned this week, but I think I can move most of them back a week or two . . ." She realized she was rambling, and Sarah didn't need to hear the minutiae of her work life. Changing the subject as quickly as she could, Mallory said, "Maybe you and I can take some time together this trip? Lunch on Monday?"

"Um, Mallory, can you hold on a minute? Let me close the door . . . okay, you still there?"

Mallory could hear worry in her voice.

"Yes. And I'm not going anywhere. What's up?"

Sarah lowered her voice, as if hiding in her office wasn't good enough. "Things have gotten very strange. Matt is doing a lot of unexpected buying and selling."

"Of the art? That has to be good for you," said Mallory. "Don't you earn a commission either way?"

"I do in theory, but here's what's odd, and it worries me. He has me bidding on and purchasing very expensive paintings and drawings right now. He's so intent on this that it's close to absurd, like in a panic.

"I'll give you an example. Two of the major auction houses here in New York are handling the sale of a famous collection, and Matt is insisting I bid on three pieces that could go for fifty million or more."

"I still don't see the problem, Sarah."

"The art you saw the night you were there, which was the Frankenthaler, the Olitski, and a Jasper Johns that I recently purchased for him, have disappeared. They're gone."

"You don't mean stolen?"

"No, no. He's sold those to someone else, *but not through my gallery.*"

"Ah, I see what you're saying. Another gallery has muscled in on your territory. Is that it?"

Sarah ignored the question. "What's really odd is that Matt had insisted he loved those artists and their work and that's why he was buying it. Now it's gone. I was told by the housekeeper he had the security guys pack it all up and send it off to the new owners, whoever they are. Like overnight that happened."

Mallory hesitated before saying, "So the Brinkerhoff Collection is really just about impressing people? Is that it? He isn't the first, you know. I see plenty of Teslas among my clients."

"Not sure. People were plenty impressed with what he had before. Maybe it's because this new collection that's on the auction block belonged to one of the world's richest men. Maybe he likes being compared to that guy," said Sarah, thinking out loud.

"He wouldn't be the first. It's the way some men use their wealth to bolster their ego."

"I know you're right. But why doesn't he let *me* sell it if that's what he wants? I mean, I could be making a lot of money for both of us."

Mallory checked her watch. She was anxious to get her run in before the sun got too high.

"Let's have lunch and talk about it," said Mallory. "Maybe I can come up with a strategy you can use to persuade him to give you the business."

"Okay. You're making me feel a little better," said Sarah. "My flight gets in to Rhinelander tomorrow night late. Will you be at your dad's?"

*   *   *

Off the phone with Sarah, Mallory called Osborne. She knew he never minded when she stayed at his house, but she should at least let him know she might show up.

"Hey, Dad, looks like I'm on your doorstep late Monday morning. My client, Matt Brinkerhoff, just ruined my weekend with the news that I have a Monday meeting with him up there at the Hemlock Lake place. Sorry."

"Not to worry," said Osborne, "you know where the key is. I won't be home until late in the afternoon."

"Going fishing?" asked Mallory with a smile.

"Not exactly," said her father. "One of Lew's Wausau boys has volunteered to take a few hours Sunday and help me find some files that might help on a cold case that the sheriff's department is working. These are files that haven't been seen in forty years, so it's like the files from my dental practice, and you know how I hid those."

Mallory laughed. "Honestly, Dad, I'll never forget how you maneuvered around Mom. She never did find out, did she?"

Chapter Twenty

No, Osborne's wife, Mary Lee, never had found out where and how he had stashed his old files—she would not have approved. When Osborne sold his dental practice, he had been determined to save his files of patients who would not be continuing with the dentist who had purchased his practice. The files held a history of the dental practice he and his father had shared. It was a history that went beyond the dental chair; it was a chronicle of their lives together. And the lives of many of their friends, some of whom had passed on. Lives passed on, but memories didn't, and Osborne did not want to lose those.

Osborne's mother had died when he was six years old. Overwhelmed and grief stricken, his father had sent the young boy off to a Jesuit boarding school in southern Wisconsin. But even with that distance between them, the father and son stayed close, a closeness that would stabilize Osborne in his adult years.

Perhaps because he'd grown up without a marriage to observe, he hadn't questioned the distance that developed between him and Mary Lee, the woman he married in his early twenties. Osborne didn't realize until two days after their wedding that they might be a bad fit. She spent their wedding night sitting on the floor of their hotel room counting all the cash they had received as wedding gifts. But it was too late, as he had been raised to be a man of his word. Soon she was criticizing what he wore, insisting he go to dinner parties hosted by her friends from the country club, and sniffing with distaste when he suggested they host his friends from fishing and deer hunting along with their wives. "I don't really know those people, Paul," she would say. That translated to "I don't *want* to know those people, Paul." And he got the message.

While he wondered if all wives were so controlling, he soon heard enough complaints from his fishing buddies about their wives' behaviors that he realized he wasn't alone in his feelings, that few couples seemed to have it better.

It wasn't until he met Lewellyn Ferris that he discovered a secret that changed his life: the woman who captures your heart with her looks and her voice and her body can also be your best friend.

Mary Lee had not been his best friend. She was his boss. She ran the house, the family, their social life. Only his time in the boat was safe from her dictates.

And so it was that he learned early to stay out of her way when it came to purchasing furniture and making decisions on the decor of their home, especially when they built the lake house. Every inch of that house was built to Mary Lee's specifications.

When Osborne officially retired and said he wanted to keep his old oak file cabinet with the records of his and his father's patients, Mary Lee, determined to see those files in the trash, wasted no words. "Paul, they're clutter. We don't need clutter. Those dumb files will take up space that I can use for a new credenza to hold my table linens."

The only thing she despised more than his files was the money he spent on fishing gear. Well, not the only thing. She had also hated the fact that he insisted on practicing dentistry in Loon Lake, as his father had before him, when she knew he could be making much more money and "really improving" their lifestyle if he would open a practice in Milwaukee. That badgering went on for a decade before she grudgingly gave up.

When the construction of their new house was completed, Osborne had only one place on their property he could retreat to in peace: his fish-cleaning shed. It was a small space, but it had electricity and running water. More important, he could call it his own. The blessing was that the shed was attached to the back of their garage and safely out of Mary Lee's line of sight.

With help from Ray Pradt, who lived in a trailer home (also on Mary Lee's hate list but nothing she could do anything about), he managed to build a small but tidy addition to the fish-cleaning shed. Working together, Osborne and Ray hid the new room behind a false front of garage storage units. They made it large enough to hold the two antique oak filing cabinets packed with his dental files as well as the old wooden desk and chair, which he had saved from the back room of his dental office.

With that, a major marital issue was resolved: Mary Lee had no decorating plans for storage units in a garage she rarely entered. The very thought of the fish-cleaning shed allegedly caused her "to break out in hives," which meant the entrance to Osborne's hidden sanctum was safe.

* * *

Sunday morning Osborne drove down to Wausau, where Bruce Peters met him at the entrance to the newly completed Wausau Crime Lab. Bruce gave him a quick tour, pointing out how the new building was much larger and better equipped than the old one. Together they walked down to the original building, which was scheduled for a demolition that had not yet begun.

"Bruce, thank you for taking the time this morning," said Osborne as Bruce unlocked the entrance to the old lab building.

"Not a problem, Doc. I have to be in Madison for a seminar starting tomorrow, so I'm happy to get this taken care of. It may not surprise you to hear I'm pretty darn interested myself in what we might find."

"You know, I was down here often back when Dr. Nystrom was running the autopsy room. I remember his office was down this hallway," said Osborne, leading the way. He stopped at an open door and peered in. "This is it, but what is this? A library?"

"Yes," said Bruce, "I thought you knew that. This has been used for textbooks and research manuals for a good ten years or longer. The change was made just before I got here."

"Guess I'm old school, hey?" said Osborne with a chuckle.

After poking around for a few minutes, Bruce pointed to a space behind a freestanding bookcase. "Looks like a closet back in here. I'll check it out." Opening the door, he peered into the dark space, searching for a light. Osborne lingered behind him, hoping to hear good news. "More boxes," Bruce called out, his voice muffled. "Oh, wait, there's a cabinet back in the corner."

Osborne, still hopeful, crowded into the closet behind Bruce. He watched as the cabinet door swung open to expose two shelves with trays filled with manila envelopes. Kneeling, Bruce pulled one tray out, studied the writing on an envelope, and looked up at Osborne. "Names and dates, Doc. Keep your fingers crossed. We may have found the slides."

After setting the trays on an old Formica-topped desk in the middle of the room, Osborne and Bruce each took a tray and started going through the envelopes.

"I have the Hanson file in my office," said Bruce. "It's the one I copied and emailed to Judith. Now . . ." He shuffled through the envelopes, talking to himself. "If we can match the name of Margaret Hanson to one of these . . . hey, got it. Dated on July 17, 1967."

"Has to be it," said Osborne. He watched as Bruce opened the envelope and slid the contents onto the table-top. The two men grinned at each other.

"Score," said Bruce.

"You did it," said Osborne as he reached into his pocket for his cell phone. "Lew?" He got her voice mail, but before he could leave a message, she called back. "Lew," he repeated, while Bruce continued to look through the contents of the envelope. "Good, news: Bruce found the microscopic slides from Roger Nystrom's files. Are you okay if I ask Bruce to see if the DNA can be sourced from these? We don't know what the cost will be."

"Fine, Doc," said Lew. "I'm deputizing you immediately to work on this investigation. Come in and sign the paperwork for me when you get back, okay?"

Phone off, Osborne nodded to Bruce. "We have the green light. Now let's hope we can find someone who can work with these. Any thoughts?"

Bruce, who was famous for his bushy, expressive eyebrows, raised them in glee as he said, "Do I ever! I'm fishing the Prairie River outside of Gleason tonight with a good buddy who's a microbiologist over at the hospital. I'll bet you if anyone can access the contents, he can. If he can't, I'll be he knows someone in the field who can. His specialty is forensic microbiology, and we're hoping to get a budget increase so we can hire the guy. I'll check with him and let you know."

"A timeline too?" asked Osborne. "I know Lew is hoping this doesn't take more than a few weeks. Judith Hanson needs closure after what she's learned of her sister's death. The sooner the better."

"I understand," said Bruce. "I'll let you know after I talk with my buddy Jake tonight."

Chapter
Twenty-One

Sarah looked down at the unfamiliar number on her cell phone. The call had come in while she was talking to Mallory Osborne. A new client? She recognized the area code from the calls she had gotten from Matt Brinkerhoff or one of his assistants. Though she was surprised the caller had not left a voice mail, she returned the call.

"Hello, Sarah, thank you for calling back." The woman's voice sounded vaguely familiar.

"You're welcome, but who is this?"

"Oh, sorry, Sarah, I forgot you wouldn't recognize my number. This is Alex Brinkerhoff, and I'm here in the city at our company apartment. I need you to stop by for a few minutes. I have something to show you. The apartment is in Murray Hill near the Midtown Tunnel. Shouldn't take more than twenty minutes from your gallery. How soon can you get here?"

Sarah was taken aback. She knew from comments Matt had dropped that he was going through a divorce.

The last thing she wanted was to get in the middle of a property dispute. She decided to play dumb.

"No, I can't do this right now. I'm sorry. I have someone coming in to see a painting shortly. But I fly out to Rhinelander late tomorrow. Will you be back at the Hemlock Lake house tomorrow or later this week? I'm there until Wednesday afternoon. Maybe we can talk then?"

Silence. The woman's voice hardened as she said, "No, we need to talk *now*. I told you I'm over in Murray Hill and I expect to see you within the hour." The words might have been innocent, but the threat was unmistakable.

Half an hour later, Sarah gave her name to the doorman at the elegant brownstone and waited until he was told to let her in.

"Good. Come in, Sarah," said Alex as she opened the door to the apartment. "Follow me." She was dressed in jeans and a well-worn sweatshirt. No makeup, and her blond curls were tucked behind her ears. "We'll keep this short."

Sarah followed her down a short hallway and into a small living room, where paintings and drawings of all sizes had been stacked against a black sofa and two black upholstered chairs. One swift glance told Sarah she was looking at twenty or more artworks standing side by side on the floor. One at the front of one stack alarmed her: a work by Jean-Michel Basquiat that she had sold to Matt a month earlier for $37 million. A wave of nausea swept through her. She wanted desperately to sit down and get hold of herself.

"What on earth?" she asked, squeaking the words out as she turned to Alex. The woman was sitting on one arm of the sofa, her arms crossed across her chest as she watched Sarah.

"I'm getting an emergency divorce," she said. "I plan to be far away when the shit hits the fan, but I like you, Sarah. I don't think you have any idea what Matt is involved in, so this is a warning."

"What you're talking about?" asked Sarah. "I buy and sell art for your husband. That's all." Uncomfortable standing alone in the middle of the room, she found a credenza to lean against. She stared back at Alex, who was about ten feet away.

Alex dropped her head as if thinking hard, then raised her eyes to Sarah's as she said, "Matt doesn't love art. What he's been doing is embezzling money from investors in his hedge fund and using it to buy the art from you. Then he sells it to a third party who will hide the money out of the country."

"You're telling that your husband is laundering stolen money through the art?"

"It didn't start that way. At first he was very taken with you and the art and . . . everything." She waved a hand. "Then his major backers, a group of Chinese businessmen who put millions into the hedge fund, announced they were backing out of their commitment. That was six weeks ago. Meantime the competition in the cybersecurity field had gotten fierce. Matt panicked. That's when this all started."

She went on. "That's why he won't let you sell it for him. This way the feds can't trace what he's doing. Only he made one more huge mistake."

Sarah waited for the woman with the white-blond curls and the freckled face to say more. She noticed again the large but fading bruise under her left eye and cheekbone.

"He got himself a girlfriend. He didn't think I'd find out, but he picked a woman who had a bad habit of saying she was 'Mrs. Matthew Brinkerhoff' when she was shopping for clothes at the same store where I shop. Her purchases were delivered to my home by mistake.

"She isn't the first one he's cheated with, but this time the timing was bad. I'll put up with the women, but I won't be a party to his rotten scheme. That's why the emergency divorce: I am determined to be out of the picture legally before he's caught."

Sarah, too stunned to say anything, sat in silence while Alex jumped to her feet and paced across the room in front of the stacked art works. "I hate his guts. He's ruined my life, and now he's stealing money from friends—and family too. All these people who have trusted him with their money. Even my parents gave him their life savings!"

"How long have you been married to him? Did you know he was capable of this?"

"Of stealing? Or of hitting me?" She raised a hand to her face. "We got married four years ago. I'm Matt's third wife. Something I didn't realize until it happened a second time—since at first I thought he had slipped and hit me by accident—is that Matt is mean. Just plain mean. So stay out of his way."

She stared at Sarah, who realized she had better say something. "Um, I know the big auction houses and art galleries are aware of the money laundering risks. I'm . . . I'm really surprised your husband . . . um, your ex . . . doesn't' know that." She wished to hell she could stop stuttering. "Tell me one thing, Alex. What makes him think he can get away with this?"

Alex leaned forward. She enunciated every word as she said, "Matthew Brinkerhoff thinks he is so smart, smarter that everyone else. But he's going to get caught one of these days, and I don't plan to be there. Sarah, I don't want you to get caught too. You have a young family; your intentions have been good from the moment you met Matt."

Sarah didn't have to ask the next question. It was becoming obvious Alex was planning to turn Matt in to the federal authorities.

"I know what you're thinking, and you are absolutely right," said Alex with a smirk. "But I want my money first. It won't be a million dollars that I get, but it'll be enough. Then I plan to sit back and watch all hell break loose."

She leaned forward to speak in a conspiratorial tone. "See, he has no idea that I know about the other woman—or that I know what he's up to with the money. I didn't tell him I got his hooker's packages. I returned those and gave the store her correct address, which I got from the phone." Again the smirk. "He has no idea I know about her. And the money laundering? How do I know about that?"

"I imagine . . . what . . . someone on his staff told you?"

"No. When you stay at the Hemlock Lake house, keep your ears open. I mean that literally. The builder short-changed us on the construction with shoddy materials. You can hear *everything* through the bedroom walls.

"I sat in bed one night when he was on the phone in his office, which is right next to the master bedroom, and listened to him tell the crook he's working with just how long it would take him to get the money out of the hedge fund, buy the art, have it shipped, and hand it over to that bozo."

"Does he know that you're aware of that? Is that why he hit you?"

"He slugged me when I told him I wanted a divorce. I wasn't surprised. Guess I should have ducked, huh?"

"Does your son know you're filing for divorce?"

"That little creep? Barry's from Matt's first marriage. We don't have children, thank goodness. I can't stand that kid. When I'm there, he stays with his mother over in Three Lakes. I have to say, Matt and that kid of his are two of a kind. I'm not surprised he hurt that girl the way he did, and I hope he goes to jail for a good long time."

"This is awful, Alex," said Sarah, shaking her head in despair. "Just awful. I'm not sure what to do. I wish you hadn't told me." She gave a rueful smile. "Of course, I don't mean that. I'm lucky you've been good enough to warn me."

"I like you."

"You don't even know me. Not really."

"But I do. We talked, remember? You're honest, Sarah; more than that, I've seen the art you've chosen for Matt. And I've seen how and why you've chosen it. Reasons that go beyond money. That tells me who you are.

"One more thing. I was watching the other night when Matt came on to you and how you handled that. Given his reputation and his money, not all women would have turned him down. I didn't, and look where it got me." She grimaced. "You did. I respect that—no, I *appreciate* that."

Sarah spoke up. "I have a family, a husband and two children."

"So you said. Still, you know what I mean."

Sarah glanced around the room and all the stacked artworks. "What happens next?"

"People are coming to pack these up, and my lawyer is handing it all over to the authorities. Matt thinks it's being sent to him, but I'll say something caused a delay.

"Sarah, please keep everything I've told you confidential until later in the week. That's when my legal team will take action. I'll let you more when I can. Right now I'm here to get a few of my personal things, and then I'm gone."

Alex stood up as she said, "Now, if you'll excuse me, I need to finish up here. Do you mind letting yourself out?"

Looking over the stacks of art, Sarah felt sick to her stomach again. Still sitting on the end table, she went over what meager options she had. *If* she had any.

"Alex—"

"What?"

"I'm canceling my trip to Wisconsin. I can't do this."

"No, please, go. If you don't go, you'll tip him off before my lawyer and I have everything lined up with the feds. He'll leave the country with all those wonderful paintings, and it'll be too late to stop him.

"Sarah, you'll be fine. Especially now that I've alerted you and you can take steps to save your gallery's investments. But that can't happen if Matt finds out too soon. You have my cell number and I have yours. I will keep you updated on what's happening on my end. And you do the same for me, please? We'll want to know who Matt is seeing and when. All right?"

"Okay, but I'll shorten my trip. I'll be there for the Monday meeting and fly back the next morning. I'll feel a lot safer doing that."

After deciding to go ahead with the trip to Wisconsin, Sarah thought about how she might be able to salvage some of the art while she was out there. Maybe store a few of the small paintings at Dr. Osborne's house? That might be difficult.

On the other hand, the trip would give her an excuse to avoid bidding on the three very expensive paintings, the ones Matt had said he wanted, until her return. If she could accomplish just that much and then get back to NYC, she could then sever the gallery's relationship with Matt. That way, maybe she could avoid having the gallery go bankrupt, not to mention getting herself arrested for being part of the scam.

Oh God, just being *connected* to Matt and his money laundering could ruin her business. Damn it. She would talk to Mallory's father and his friend the sheriff. Maybe they could help. At least she knew she had a safe place to hide if she had to.

Her mind made up, she was getting to her feet when Alex came back into the room. Opening the apartment door for Sarah to leave, Alex said, "Be careful, Sarah. Matt has one rule: people are expendable."

Chapter
Twenty-Two

Judith woke to the patter of raindrops on the bedroom window. She checked her clock radio. Jumping out of bed, she pulled on sweats and a light sweatshirt. If she hurried, she could make seven-thirty Mass at St. Mary's.

Early-Sunday Mass with her father had been a treasured habit of her childhood. Smiling to herself as she drove over, she had a flash of feeling young again, certainly younger than her sixties.

She was pleased to see that the pew that had "belonged" to her family was empty. After genuflecting, she slipped in, knelt, and prayed as all the ritual prayers of her youth came flooding back word for word.

After taking Communion herself, she watched the other parishioners file by. One, to her surprise, was Dr. Paul Osborne. She was surprised, too, to find him waiting for her outside the church.

"Good morning, Judith," he said with a shake of her hand, "good to see you. Hope I don't ruin your day, but

I have a tip to pass along if you have a moment. It has to do with Camp Ashwabagon." Osborne watched her face, knowing he was referring to her sister's death and hoping she wouldn't find the mention depressing.

"Love to hear it," said Judith, responding with enthusiasm. "I've been planning to visit the Loon Lake Historical Society Museum and see if they may have references to the camp. I would love to find out if anyone from those days might still be alive, though I'm sure that's a long shot. Didn't the camp close back in the eighties?"

"Yes. But I'm sure you'll find information on the camp at the museum. They have a room dedicated to the summer camps that flourished up here from the 1920s on."

"That far back? I didn't know that."

"People forget this region was the center of logging in the late 1880s. Fortunes were made up here, which is why we have so many people, generations later, with lake homes and cottages they've inherited.

"Sheriff Ferris and I had a meeting very recently with our local tennis coach, and he happened to mention that his grandfather taught tennis fifty years ago at Camp Ashwabagon. His name is Philip Henman, and even as he must be near ninety, his grandson said he's in good health. Unlike some of us," said Osborne with a laugh, "he appears to still have his wits about him."

"This is very helpful. Thank you, Doc," said Judith, shaking hands again and starting to walk away. "Oh, wait, do you think his grandson would mind if I called him? I'd love to have a chat with his grandfather if he thinks that would be okay."

"I doubt he would mind. The grandson is Bob Henman. His father-in-law is one of my best friends. I'll get a phone number for you. And by the way, did you know the historical society keeps their museum open weekends throughout the summer?"

Checking online while chewing her second piece of cinnamon toast, Judith saw that the museum would open at eleven that morning. After rummaging through the old wooden desk still in the room that had been her father's den, she found a pad of paper she could use to take notes.

As she got up from the desk, her eyes rested on the gun cabinet in the corner. While she had emptied her parents' closets of their belongings immediately after her mother's death, she hadn't touched items like her father's guns or her mother's antique furniture and linens. They were objects filled with memories that she loved holding on to.

The guns were a 12-gauge and a 20-gauge, which she had learned to use when she was a teenager. Even into her twenties, she would drive up to spend a weekend bird hunting with her grandfather. She had been a good shot, so they always returned with a partridge or two, which her mother would prepare with wild rice.

Judith smiled to herself as she remembered the route they walked during those fall days. The land had been perfect for bird hunting, with stands of young aspens along old logging trails. Hard to find a better place to scout partridge.

Judith looked out the kitchen window to see how hard it was raining. If it let up later, she might take a walk. *Down memory lane*, she thought. The area they had hunted had been on the southeast side of Hemlock Lake and just off the public landing. Of course, the landing might have been moved, but those woods were owned by the state, so they had to be as pristine today as they had been years ago.

"Good," Judith said to herself, standing up and walking over to put her dishes in the sink. "I have a plan. First the museum and then a good, long walk." This was why she loved Sundays.

Chapter
Twenty-Three

～

Arriving at the Loon Lake Historical Society Museum, Judith sauntered through the first three rooms, which were filled with logging memorabilia, including framed photos of the logging trains and the men who had worked the woods. It was in a side room where she found the information on more than twenty summer camps that had been popular in their day. Some of the names she remembered from when she was growing up. Camp Birchrock was her Girl Scout camp. Then there was Camp Deerhorn outside Rhinelander; Camp Ojibwa near Eagle River; Camp Tesomas, the Boy Scout camp; Camp Bryn Afon; and many more.

She moved through the room slowly, checking the names on various booklets and albums. Then she found them: a set of summer "yearbooks" from Camp Ashwabagon, donated to the museum by the Schueppert family from Ann Arbor, Michigan.

Judith swept up the set and moved to a wide table set out in the main room especially for people wanting to peruse materials like the yearbooks. She was interested in one year in particular: 1967.

The yearbook was a photo album with handwritten descriptions of what was pictured, including some names. The album held photos of the beach and docks with dozens of rowboats and canoes. Water skiing had been popular, and there were two large diving rafts.

The onshore pictures featured a large dining room, a workshop, two tennis courts, a ball field, and a stable with horses. Listed as administrators were the camp director, his assistants, senior counselors, and the kitchen staff. Judith picked out the individual Osborne had mentioned: *Phil Henman, Tennis Instructor.*

Judith studied the picture of the young man standing in front of the nets on the tennis court. He couldn't be much over twenty, maybe twenty-five at the oldest. Maybe, maybe, maybe, she hoped, he was still alive. Still alive with good memories of those years. She knew that was asking a lot.

*   *   *

By three thirty, the rain had eased. At four the sun came out and the temperature was a lovely sixty-five. Grabbing her rain jacket and hat just in case, Judith got into her SUV and headed out of town. She knew the route to Hemlock Lake by heart, even though it was a few miles out of town.

She eased down the county road, hoping to see the access road to the boat landing. *Whoa.* She slowed down and signaled. Not only was the road there, but it had a large sign pointing in the direction for parking after unloading a boat trailer. *Whew.*

Her heart was light as she trudged up the hill away from the loading docks. She followed a deer trail into the nearby woods and trudged a good quarter mile until she stumbled on faint markings underfoot, which were all that remained of the logging lane she had walked so many years before. It did not appear to be well used, though she suspected a few deer hunters might have driven their ATVs down it looking for deer rubs, evidence of big bucks hiding among the trees.

She was twenty minutes down the old logging lane when she made another heartwarming discovery: the old horse trail. This was a bonanza. When she was eleven and twelve years old, her two closest friends had been Mary Kay and Jodie—sisters whose family owned a couple of quarter horses that they let the girls ride bareback.

Since Judith was enthralled with horses and horseback riding at that time in her young life, she had managed her friendships with Mary Kay and Jodie so she could bike out to their house every Saturday and join them horseback riding. So much fun.

Trudging through the brush and branches covering the horse trail, Judith made a mental note to see if her old friends were still around. She doubted that, as she was sure her mother would have mentioned any news about them. She had walked a good couple of miles when the trail opened up into the field running along the lakeshore where the horses used to be pastured. Lake Hemlock was off to the left, the water glimmering under the sun.

One thing had changed, however. Her old friends' house and barn, which had once stood close to the water's edge, were gone. Judith walked over to where she remembered the two buildings had been, but only a few shards of broken stone indicated where the foundations once stood. The pine forest had taken over.

She remembered the forest and how it stretched back for miles. Too often her father had been called out to treat a hunter who had gotten lost in dense woods and, after spending a night in the cold, was near death from hypothermia.

"That forest is so dangerous," her father had warned her. "Do not hunt in there without a compass. And be sure to tell someone where you're going and when. Don't be foolish."

She ambled down to the lake and stood on the shoreline, peering past the fringed branches of ancient white pines standing off to her right.

Ah, now she understood the reason for the disappearance of the old house and barn. Someone had built a stunning contemporary mansion on the far side of the stand of pines. No doubt the owners of the multimillion-dollar property had insisted on a perfect sight line, an unobscured view from the deck fronting the house. As she studied the remarkable home, she remembered that there had once been a large hunting lodge on the same location. It was one of the classic handcrafted log lodges the logging barons had built in the 1880s.

Judith turned to walk the trails back to where she had parked her car. She was glad to have found her favorite haunts. As she drove back to town, she thought over the events of the day. No answer to who had killed her sister . . . yet. But thanks to Doc Osborne, she had a clue. One clue, but that could be all she needed.

Chapter Twenty-Four

～

In the middle of Monday morning, Lew's personal cell phone rang. She chuckled at the sight of the caller's name. "You are out of line, Bruce Peters," she said with a friendly chortle. "Since when do you think I fish on a Monday? Worst day of the week in my world. Especially now. Don't let me get started on what I'm looking at on my desk this morning."

After his answering laugh, Bruce said, "Just calling to alert you to information on the DNA sample I'm pursuing. It may take some time to find a lab that has the technology to work with the slides."

"I understand," said Lew. "Doc told me you two had found Dr. Nystrom's slides and turned the evidence from the Hanson case over to your friend the microbiologist. Is this good news? Was he able to get a DNA sample?"

"No. He said it's such a recent development in the technology around cold case evidence that there are few labs able to work with it. But my friend is checking with forensic microbiologists he knows. He's confident we'll locate the right lab sometime in the next few days.

"Meanwhile, I am sending along the DNA sample we have from the recent Knudsen case. As you saw in the autopsy report, the medical examiner found human skin under her fingernails. She let me know first thing this morning that the DNA analysis was completed, so the result is on the way to Dani as we speak."

Walking into Dani's office, Lew shared the news from Bruce. "I know, Sheriff Ferris," said Dani, "I got the email with all the information a few minutes ago. If you approve, I'll get that DNA search going."

"Yes, please, Dani. As soon as possible," said Lew.

"Will do," said Dani, looking excited. She loved searching for DNA matches. It was much more interesting that executing a color weave on a client at the hair salon, and the payoff was better than money. More than once an individual accused of assault or an attempt to commit murder had been exonerated thanks to her diligence. That meant a life not ruined; it meant her skill and diligence counted. Today she was confident that her search with this sample would have a critical impact on the investigation into the death of a young woman.

* * *

A soft rap on Lew's office door announced the arrival of her best friend, the tall, slim man who moved with the agility of someone used to climbing in and out of boats. Lew waved him in, saying, "Morning, Doc. Got time for one last cup of coffee?"

Osborne took his usual chair in front of her desk, then leaned forward, his eyes anxious. "Got a call from Mallory that she's driving up from Chicago this afternoon for yet another event at the Brinkerhoffs'."

"An *event* at the Brinkerhoffs'? That's odd timing. We just released the kid on bail. Hell of a time for an *event*." She had an immediate image of Matt Brinkerhoff's anger when she'd arrested his son.

"It is, and that's what she said too. She was surprised to hear about it on Saturday. She asked me if there's anything new on the court case involving Matt Brinkerhoff's son. I told her the young man has been arrested, charged, and released on bail in the custody of his mother. Any new developments?"

"Dani is doing a search on a DNA sample found on the girl's body now," said Lew. "I'll know more shortly. Shouldn't take long. We got a sample from Barry when we brought him in, so it's just a matter of the timing right now. I'll be surprised if there isn't a match.

"It's on my list to check with Martha Burns, the Knudsens' lawyer," said Lew, "although she said he'd let me know when they got the hearing scheduled. I know she was working to get it moved out of Voelker's court. She said she checked the list of donors to his recent election campaign and has good reason to allege conflict of interest on Voelker's part. Matt Brinkerhoff was the largest donor to his campaign. Why does Mallory want to know?"

"She had a call from her friend Sarah, who is very concerned about something going on out at the Brinkerhoffs'. Mallory's meeting Sarah for lunch today and should know more."

"Why would a gallery owner be concerned with that family situation? Matt's not the one likely to go to prison."

"Good question," said Osborne. "Very good question. I'll know more soon. On a happier note, Ray came by early this morning to report he had a very nice Saturday instructing Dani and her girlfriend on the benefits of life among the walleye. He's arranged to take Dani out one more time, maybe this evening. He said she's an enthusiastic student."

Lew gave Osborne the dim eye as she said, half joking, "Does Ray Pradt ever have a bad time when surrounded by the opposite sex? I mean, really, Doc."

"He also said he might ask your young colleague out for dinner sometime. I thought you should know."

"Dinner?" said Lew. "We know how that's likely to end. Well, Dani is a big girl. Once she finds out it's impossible to get Ray to commit to anything long term, I hope they can stay friends. I don't need conflict between two of the people who do valuable work for this department.

I got enough trouble now that I'm trying to hire two new police chiefs."

Osborne shook his head. "Maybe Dani will lose interest. She strikes me as the type of young woman who needs a more traditional man in her life. And Ray Pradt is not traditional."

"No he is not," said Lew. "I happen to like him as he is, bad habits and all." She waved her empty coffee cup at Osborne. "You better get out of here, Doc, I have a job to do."

Watching the man with whom she loved to share her morning coffee walk out of her office, she thought of her comment on Ray: *bad habits and all*. She hadn't meant that literally, and she knew Osborne knew it too.

* * *

Ray's worst habit had not been his obsession over fishing muskies but his drinking. Though his and Osborne's lives were very different, at one point they had spiraled down a parallel path into alcoholism.

For Osborne it had been the loneliness and loss of everyday routines that hit after the unexpected death of Mary Lee. In spite of thirty years of an unhappy marriage, he was so used to her crabby ways and the structure she brought to his life that her death had unmoored him. Only an intervention staged by his daughters saved his life.

Ray's slide into alcoholism had been more subtle, starting in his teens, when he had made it a habit to hang out with whomever he had just been hunting or fishing with. Problem was, that habit always included a local tavern, where he soon learned why drinking was known as Wisconsin's state sport.

And so it was that two men, thirty years apart in age but equally skilled with the spinning rod, had found themselves knocking on the door with the coffeepot on the window: the meeting room for Alcoholics Anonymous.

"Well, hello, neighbor," one said to the other as they took chairs next to each other.

"Yep, hello."

From that day on, the two had driven together to their weekly meetings. One lived in a house overdecorated by his late wife, the other in a trailer home painted neon green with gaping teeth designed to look like a leaping muskie. Two very different people with a friendship forged in grief and a mutual passion for the woods and waters surrounding them.

*   *   *

Late that afternoon, Dani sat back, satisfied. Her DNA search on the sample sent by Bruce Peters had turned out much better than she'd expected.

When the match to the crime lab's DNA sample appeared on her screen, she recognized the family name:

Brinkerhoff. Assuming the DNA sample was connected to Lew's investigation of the supposed Jet Ski accident that had killed the Knudsen girl, she was intrigued. She knew Lew had fired Chief Alan Stern over his handling of the case.

Ah, thought Dani as she scrolled through the details of the note, *Lew will be very interested in that fact.* This could be big. Confirming that Barry Brinkerhoff's DNA matched the DNA found on the girl's body meant Chief Stern had made a very serious mistake. He might be in deep legal trouble too.

She shut down her computer feeling, she had accomplished a good day's work: one DNA search that had led to not one but *two* bad actors—the Brinkerhoff kid and the Deer Haven Chief of Police.

Chapter
Twenty-Five

Judith parked and walked into the house. She was debating whether or not to try reach Philip Henman, the elderly grandfather of Bob Henman. She had been able to locate a cell number for the younger man easily, as he promoted his tennis program on the Loon Lake High School website. She checked her watch. Oh well, worth a try.

She got voice mail and left a message that she was doing research on the Northwoods historic summer camps. "Dr. Paul Osborne told me that the elder Mr. Henman might be able to help me out, as I would love to get some background information on Camp Ashwabagon.

"Is there any chance of reaching Mr. Henman? Here's my phone number, and please let him know I would be happy to meet with him in person, if that's at all possible. I work at the McBride County Sheriff's Department, so I can be reached there too. Thank you for helping me out with this project. Again, I'm Judith Hanson, and

I recently moved back to the area. Here's my number again . . . good-bye."

After leaving her number, Judith thought back over the long message she had left. She hoped that mentioning where she was employed would add legitimacy to her request, maybe encourage someone to get back to her.

Less than five minutes after her call, her cell phone rang. "Is this Judith Hanson?" asked a female voice. "I'm Sandy Henman, Bob's wife, and I just listened to your message. Bob's teaching right now, so I thought I'd return your call."

"Thank you for getting back to me so quickly," said Judith.

"No problem. My grandfather-in-law is sitting here with me, and he would love to meet with you. He has quite the stories from his days at the camp."

"Wonderful," said Judith. "I don't imagine this evening would work for me to stop by? I could introduce myself, and then we could set up a longer time to get together." She could hear a murmur of voices as the woman checked with Phil.

"Are you in Loon Lake?' asked the woman, back on the phone. "We live just north of town on Shepard Lake right off the highway, if that sounds convenient. I know Phil would love to meet with you." She dropped her voice to a whisper as she said, "He doesn't have too much going on, and visitors make his day."

"Well, it's a little after five right now. How about I come by at six thirty? But only if you'll be sure to tell me if I'm staying too long."

"See you at six thirty, and here's our address . . ."

Judith could not believe her luck. She reminded herself to be careful and not badger the old man too long. Again she hoped against hope that he still had his memory.

While grabbing a bite to eat, she went over the notes she had taken while paging through the Camp Ashwabagon yearbooks. She studied the pages so intently that by the time she finished, it felt like she'd been on the place in person. At six fifteen, she gathered up the yearbook for 1967 and headed out the door to her car.

Ten minutes later she parked in front of the Henmans' house, a handsome wood frame house with a tennis court in what should have been the front yard. She stepped up the few steps onto a small deck and rang their front door bell. An elderly man answered. "Are you Judith?"

"Yes. May I assume you are Mr. Henman?"

"You may indeed, and the name is Phil. This is my grandson's home, but I stay here in the summer."

"Phil, you are so kind to take this time with me," she said as they shook hands. He held the door open and beckoned for her to enter.

"I'm looking forward to it," he said graciously. "Follow me out to the back deck. It's a beautiful evening, and we can watch the ducks go by while we to talk."

Half an hour into listening to Phil Henman's favorite reminiscences, Judith brought up the 1960s. "Am I correct that you started teaching at Camp Ashwabagon in the early sixties, Phil? How old were you then?"

"I was a junior in college and the top player on our tennis team," he said proudly. "The camp director recruited me after seeing me in a tournament where one of his sons was playing. His boy was in charge of the camps program, and I was hired to be his assistant. Boy, that was a learning experience."

"How so? Long hours?" asked Judith.

"Not that so much. It was the campers. All boys and all from very wealthy families out of Chicago and Detroit. Those boys would not take direction. They were out of control—by my standards, anyway. We had two of 'em arrive at camp with drugs in their suitcases."

"Drugs?" Judith was taken aback.

"Yeah, the Brinkerhoff kid had marijuana and cocaine. His buddy tried smuggling in tequila. We nailed those two right away. I wanted to send them packing, but the director wouldn't let us. He said Brinkerhoffs had been coming to Ashwabagon since it opened and he knew the boys would settle down."

"I'm sure they did," said Judith agreeably. "Wasn't there some scandal later in the sixties?"

"Sure was," said Phil, adjusting himself in his chair as if ready to tell a good story. "That damn Brinkerhoff was one of the ones involved too. Sad story. Some young girl got killed in a car accident with three of the counselors. Junior counselors they were. That time we did send them home."

"And it was a Brinkerhoff again?"

"Yeah, Matt was one; then there was Jerry Imus and Fred Perryman. Three of them. My understanding was that all four had been with a party of teenagers drinking at someone's cottage. The girl drove off with the three boys. I heard the car rolled, she was thrown out and died of a broken neck." While he was talking, Judith jotted down the names of the three counselors—the names that had been redacted in the autopsy report on her sister's death.

"Wow, is that what the police said?" Judith feigned innocence.

"That's what I heard from the camp director. This was right at the end of summer that year. I was leaving to go back to the college where I was coaching in those days. Never heard any more about it. That was my last summer teaching there."

Judith lingered another hour with questions until she saw the elderly man was tiring. She got to her feet, saying, "Phil, I appreciate your time today. I'll keep you posted on what I do with this information I'm collecting."

"You do that. Say, you should know that Matt Brinkerhoff is still around here. He built himself some fancy summer home over on Hemlock Lake. Oh, wait, you're working in the sheriff's department, so you must have heard about his kid getting arrested. Bob told me about it this morning."

"Yes, I'm familiar with that situation," said Judith. "As you can imagine, it's been very hard on the Knudsen family. Afraid that's all I can say about it right now, Phil, as the investigation is still underway."

Phil nodded. "The girl took tennis lessons from Bob. He's pretty upset with this. We all think Matt Brinkerhoff has enough money to get that kid off too."

"You think so?"

"Happens all the time," said the old man, nodding with the wisdom of age and experience. "Happens all the time. Can drive you nuts."

Chapter
Twenty-Six

Hunched over the kitchen table in her father's house, Mallory checked her phone for the umpteenth time. Then she stood up to stare out the window over the sink, willing the arrival of Osborne's black Subaru. Empty driveway, darn. Okay, how about Lew's cruiser? If only *someone* would get home. She sat back down and picked up her phone.

Lew pulled into the driveway first, and Mallory jumped up to open the back door. "Oh, Lew, I'm so worried," she said, watching as Lew unbuckled her belt to lay her holster and Sig Sauer 9mm pistol on the shelf over the clothes dryer, where it would be safe from Mike the dog but easy to reach in an emergency.

For reasons she didn't quite understand, the sight of Lewellyn Ferris never failed to make Mallory feel safe. Not angry that her widowed father had found a woman to love, not jealous that he spent more time with her than with his daughters. Just plain safe.

Lew Ferris wasn't beautiful, not even pretty. She looked, if anything, wholesome. Broad across the shoulders, with firm breasts and a sturdy torso, she was a woman who looked strong enough to raise the front end of a car. Well, not *that* strong, Mallory thought, but she looked like she could hold her own in a confrontation with any threat short of a black bear. At the moment, just the sight of Lewellyn Ferris was reassuring.

* * *

Less than two minutes later, Osborne's car pulled in. "Oh, good, here's Dad," said Mallory, her voice full of relief.

"What's wrong, Mallory?" asked Lew after walking into the kitchen and pouring herself a glass of water. She motioned for Mallory to sit down at the kitchen table. "You look like your best friend died."

Before Mallory could answer, Osborne joined them in the kitchen, smiling at the sight of his daughter. "What time did you get here?"

"Dad, sit down," said Mallory, ignoring the question. "My friend Sarah is in serious trouble. She needs help." Her voice trembled.

Watching Osborne's daughter as she motioned for them to join her at the kitchen table, Lew was taken aback. She had never seen Mallory so shaken. Trying to calm her down, Lew said, "I'm sure we can help. Just tell us what the problem is."

"The man Sarah has been buying all that art for?" Mallory's words rushed out. "He's—"

"He's assaulted her," said Lew, finishing Mallory's sentence while reaching for her cell phone.

"No, no," said Mallory, "worse. I mean, maybe not worse, but just as bad—"

"Take a deep breath," said Lew, as Osborne walked over to put his hands on his daughter's shoulders.

"He's laundering money through that art. He's stealing from his investors and hiding the money in the art, which he's shipping out of the country. Sarah just found out. She's terrified he'll find out she knows."

"Stop. Back up," said Lew, raising both her hands. "How *does* she know this?"

"Alex told her."

"Alex? Who's Alex?"

"Matt Brinkerhoff's wife. Ex-wife. She's getting an emergency divorce so she won't be tied in to any of it. Sarah met with her in New York Saturday. That's when she found out. Alex told Sarah not to say anything to anyone until she's got her divorce. Sarah's convinced she's waiting until then to blow the whistle. But Sarah thinks that'll be too late. Matt will be out of the country; the art will have disappeared and Sarah's reputation will be ruined."

"A soon-to-be ex-wife isn't always the best source," said Lew. "Where is Sarah right now?"

"On her way back to the Brinkerhoffs' over on Hemlock Lake. We met in Rhinelander for a late lunch, and then she headed back there. She's staying in one of the guest rooms. She's supposed to show new clients his collection tonight. She's terrified, Lew, just terrified."

"Can you call her? Get her on your cell?"

Mallory picked her cell phone up off the table and called. Reaching Sarah, she said, "I have someone who needs to talk to you. Where are you?" Mallory looked up at Lew and relayed what her friend told her. "She's in the guest room where she's staying this trip. She's alone . . ." Mallory handed the phone over to Lew. "There's a lot of security guys hanging around that place."

Lew took the phone. "Hello, Sarah? This is Sheriff Ferris. I have some yes and no questions for you, but first—are you safe?" Lew waited, then said, "Good. Mallory told me about your situation. Do you have a way to prove that you are correct in what you told her?"

Lew's eyes met Osborne's as she spoke, and she knew he understood her questions were designed to protect Sarah on the off chance someone might be listening.

"Sarah, I will be checking with colleagues who know about situations like this. No need for you to wait on anyone else. Understand? They may not be in touch with you until late this evening or tomorrow morning. If the circumstances warrant, are you willing to go on the record?"

"Yes," said Sarah, her voice firm, "If they need me to document that a painting by Helen Frankenthaler is not a copy, I know the expert who can determine whether or not it is an original. Yes, I can reach him in the morning, I'm sure."

Lew handed the cell back to Mallory. "She got it. She'll be careful, but if what you say is true, we have to get her out of there."

"Oh my God, thank you." Mallory burst into tears, and Osborne bent to wrap his arms around her shoulders. "Oh, Dad, Sarah's such a good person, and this could devastate her family and ruin her life. I'm so worried for her." She couldn't help sobbing.

"Excuse me, you two, I have a call to make," said Lew as she walked out onto the porch. It had been six months since she had attended the seminar run by Treasury agents tracking drug money, so she knew where to start: FinCEN, the Financial Crimes Enforcement Unit. Before her call could go to voice mail, it was answered.

"Chief Ferris?" asked the male voice.

"*Sheriff* Ferris, I'm happy to say," said Lew with a chuckle, "and I may have a big one for you. Are you sitting down?"

* * *

Before walking out to her cruiser for her drive home, Lew bent over to talk to Mallory, who was still at the kitchen table, busy with her laptop. She looked up at Lew, and the expression in her eyes made clear the anxiety she was feeling for her friend. "Try to get some sleep tonight," said Lew, knowing that might be a futile suggestion. "Sarah knows who to call if she needs help. The federal agents I spoke with tonight do not need an approval or confirmation of any kind from Alex Brinkerhoff to make their move. They have enough information now to get this going."

Mallory nodded. "Thank you. I'm worried, but what else can we do?"

Lew patted her shoulder. "We'll know more in the morning." What she didn't say was that she wished Sarah Hatch had spoken with Mallory *before* flying to the Northwoods and into a risky situation.

* * *

Monday night was one of the three days a week when she and Osborne had agreed to spend their nights alone in their own homes. It was a break she needed and one that kept her feeling good about the nights she shared with him.

Doc didn't seem to mind either. It gave him time to fish late with one of his buddies before climbing into bed to read a book or relax on the sofa to watch the evening news.

And so it was that the breaks kept both of them happy and eager to be together on the other nights. Why that was, they refused to analyze. It worked. That's what counted.

Chapter
Twenty-Seven

～

Meanwhile, out on Loon Lake as the sun was setting and with Dani watching, Ray dropped his anchor in a cove protected by towering tamaracks. "This is my secret honey hole for muskie," he said to his student as he reached for his spinning rod. "And if you ever share this location with anyone, I will have to kill you."

Dani laughed, her chortle trilling across the serene surface of the lake. She was behaving as if everything Ray said was fascinating, even his dumb jokes.

And Ray, pleased she appreciated his attempts at stand-up comedy, hadn't hesitated when asked for more: "What did the fish say when he hit a concrete wall? Dam!"

Dani laughed hard, even though it might have been the third time she'd heard the joke. At the sight of satisfaction on Ray's face, she decided to gamble and ask the question that had been in the back of her mind since they'd set out that evening.

"Y'know, Ray, I'd really like to see Hemlock Lake. I hear there are really big, fancy houses on that lake. Could we fish there, maybe?"

"Sure. Tomorrow night?"

"Ooh, great. I know the Brinkerhoffs have a new house there that is just amazing. One of the girls at the salon told me about it. She does Mrs. Brinkerhoff's hair, and she had to go out there for her last appointment. She said it's very cool."

At first, he hadn't minded listening to Dani's constant chatter, so long as she kept her voice low enough that she didn't scare the fish. The evening had been enlightening.

He had watched her eyes glaze over while he was extolling the virtues of the Series 5000 Garcia Ambassadeur reels: "This particular reel keeps a fish from snapping the handle out of your hand, especially if you're a woman fishing muskies . . ." That was when he realized he had gone on too long.

The glazed eyes were a signal to give up on instruction, at least for the moment. With that, he considered that he might have to give up on Dani too. Sure, she was cute, but he was learning they might not share the same interests. Maybe some work relationships should stay work related.

"Ray, what's this?" Dani asking, looking up at him as he stood casting off the back of the boat.

"Oh, that's a fish locator. Came with the pontoon. I haven't figured out how to work it, though. I'm not good with tech stuff like that."

"Mind if I turn it on?"

"Go right ahead. If you can figure it out. I had no luck."

Minutes later he heard Dani say, "You're close. I see four fish down under there . . ."

"Are you serious?" Ray stepped down and moved to peer over her shoulder. She was right. The pontoon was hovering over the walleyes he was hoping to hook.

"Amazing. You'll have to show me how you did that," said Ray.

"Yeah? Maybe we got a trade-off going?" Dani gave Ray her best smile.

"I don't know. You don't seem too excited about fishing."

"I can grow into it," said Dani. "You take me fishing on Hemlock Lake, and I'll show you how to work your fish locater. Deal?"

"Deal," said Ray, not sure what he was getting himself into but figuring it was worth a try.

Chapter Twenty-Eight

In the midst of enjoying her breakfast before heading off to the office, Judith's cell phone rang. She picked it up and smiled: a FaceTime call from Kate and her grandchildren.

"Good morning, everyone." She walked over to fill her coffee cup, as she knew the call would last a good five minutes or longer. "Hey, Mom," said her daughter, visible in the corner of the screen, "they just listed a very nice condo two blocks from us. Evan and Lily want you to drive down and buy it."

"Hey, hey, Grandma," shouted five-year-old Evan, bouncing up and down and waving into his mom's phone. "Come see us right now and bring lots of money. Mom says the condo costs lots of money, but you will love it." Two-year-old roly-poly Lily, sitting on the floor near her big brother, burbled something Judith could not make out. The sight of the two children—Evan with his full head of brown curls, Lily with her short, straight hair as black as her mother's, and both with their mom's lively black eyes—made Judith feel so blessed. She adored those little kids.

"Hear him, Mom?" said her daughter, laughing. "Bring lots of money."

"Sounds interesting, guys," said Judith, enjoying their cheery faces. "Can't come this week, though. One of these days, I'll be down."

"Say good-bye, kids," Kate said, instructing the children. "Grandma has to go to work." She turned off the FaceTime to speak directly to her mother. "Mom, the condo is beautiful and the price is not bad."

"Thanks, sweetheart, but you know I can't come yet. Not until I know—"

"That is not healthy, and you know it, Mom. You're obsessed in a bad way. Dwelling on what happened decades ago is sick."

"Don't mince words." Judith's pleasant morning had just been ruined. "Just so you know, Kate, I have made progress. Last night I found out who the boys were that were involved in Maggie's . . . death."

"Mom, please. What on earth can you do about it anyway?" She was quiet for a second, then said, "I'm worried about you. I think you should see a therapist. Someone with a specialty in managing grief or childhood trauma. You've been living with this a very long time."

Judith sighed. "You're right. Let me think this over. Just knowing the names of the people who were there that night helps me feel better already. I'll wrap this up, I promise. Now I have to leave for the office. Give Evan and Lily a hug for me."

"Will do. Should I let that broker know you might be interested in the condo?"

Pursing her lips, Judith said, "Not yet, but keep an eye on it. Love you."

Whew, Kate was putting the pressure on. Judith knew she was right, but that didn't change her mind. She had to know more. Exactly who had done what, and why? That was all she needed to know. *Who did it and why, for God's sake?*

Chapter
Twenty-Nine

Lew had not slept well. Sarah Hatch's predicament was worrying, even if she had confidence in the federal agent with whom she had spoken. He had assured her that they would take over the investigation immediately, with Sarah's safety paramount. In a later call that evening, he'd said he had two agents lined up to be "on the road" by six the next morning.

Lew was up by five and feeling tense. As she was driving in from her farm early that morning, she spotted the faint reddening of the sumac along the roadside. She sighed; summer always ended too soon. Up behind the sumac, balsam spires pierced the pale-gold sunrise. Overhead clouds scudded across the azure promise of a new day.

She slowed to watch a wolf dart across the road. To her eye, there was no mistaking the creature for a dog. The shape of the body, the head and the legs, defined the animal, though Lew knew many people would mistake it for a large retriever. But retrievers were friendly.

After the wolf disappeared into a black spruce bog, Lew shivered and drove on. It wasn't that she didn't like wolves—that she didn't trust them. The only time she had ever gotten close to one had happened when she was out partridge hunting one afternoon. The animal, standing no more than ten yards away on the logging lane where she'd been walking, had ignored her shouts and waving arms. Instead of scampering off, the creature had stood its ground, challenging her to move forward.

Don't be stupid, she'd told herself, and backed off. Backed off, gotten back in her pickup, and driven away. She knew territorial behavior when she saw it.

Territory, she mused. With federal agents on their way to Loon Lake, she hoped to be able to help with coordinating the surveillance and arrest of their money laundering target without territory issues. It was her job to make their work run smoothly. She hoped they would accord her and her deputies the same respect.

*   *   *

She got to the courthouse and her temporary office space shortly after seven and hurried in, anxious to prepare everyone for the arrival of the federal agents. Once at her desk, she set out to review any incidents throughout the county that might have been reported the night before. Nothing major, which was good. Hearing footsteps in the hall, Lew got up from her desk. She got down the hall in time to catch Judith heading for her desk in Dani's office.

"Good morning, Judith," she said. "There's going to be a meeting in my office shortly that I would like you to be in on. Dani," she said, glancing across the room to where Dani Wright was busy on her computer, "you too. Actually, let me talk with the two of you before the others arrive. See you both in my office now, please."

Lew's tone worried Judith. Had Lew learned of her meeting with Philip Henman? Had she done something wrong by following up with him? After all, she was an administrative assistant and not a sheriff's deputy. Maybe she had violated a law?

But anything to do with Judith Hanson was the last thing on Lew Ferris's mind.

"Set everything you're working on aside," said Lew, as Dani and Judith sat themselves down in the two chairs in front of her desk. "We have an emergency. Doc Osborne's daughter, Mallory, has a close friend staying at a home on Hemlock Lake, and her life may be at risk."

Dani and Judith stared at her, speechless.

"Yes, when I say 'at risk,' I mean it," said Lew, underscoring the seriousness of what she was about to tell them. "The woman's name is Sarah Hatch. She runs an art gallery in New York City, a gallery that has been selling very expensive, very important art to a businessman whose name you've heard recently because two days ago

I arrested his son for assaulting the Knudsen girl. That man is Matthew Brinkerhoff."

"You aren't serious," said Dani, her eyes wide with amazement. "I just asked Ray to take me fishing so I could see their amazing house. Are you sure about this? My girlfriend helped his wife—"

"Let me finish," said Lew, doing her best to be polite in spite of Dani's interruption. "Sarah has learned through a family member that Matt appears to be running a money laundering scheme involving millions of dollars. I've alerted the federal agency that investigates schemes like this, and I'll be meeting with two federal agents shortly. I was notified early this morning that two agents would be flown up from Madison. I'm waiting to hear when they land at the Rhinelander airport. That should be within the hour." She checked her watch, then looked up.

"I have two priorities," said Lew. "First, Sarah Hatch is in the Brinkerhoff home, and we need to get her out. Matt does not know that she has been made aware that he is maneuvering to ship his valuable art out of the country.

"Priority number two is Matt Brinkerhoff himself. It's highly likely that he's planning to leave the country with the art. Mallory's source told her that the man has embezzled millions from his investors. He has managed to keep that information secret, but it's under investigation right now. When he learns that the feds are onto him—"

Her phone rang, and Lew checked the number. She answered, said a few words, and hung up. "The federal agents will be here in twenty minutes. I'm calling a meeting for all our county deputies and the two of you. Along with myself, you'll be coordinating the details of the operation from this location. Any questions you may have, bring them up in our next meeting. I'm sure there'll be plenty of questions."

"How do we know Sarah Hatch is okay right now?" asked Judith. She didn't like the sound of the woman being alone in a house with a man who could turn desperate.

"Doc told me that Mallory texted her early this morning and Sarah assured her that she was fine. We're hoping everything stays that way until the feds can make their move. Judith, I know you don't have law enforcement training. And we may have long hours. Are you okay working with me on this?"

Judith gave her the dim eye as she said, "Are you kidding? Try to stop me." Inappropriate though it might be, Lew couldn't help laughing.

Chapter Thirty

❧

After Dani and Judith left to return to their desks, Lew got on the phone. She wanted the meeting to include the two women along with as many of the county deputies as could make it to the courthouse within the hour. She also wanted Osborne and Mallory to answer any questions from the federal agents regarding Sarah Hatch and her safety.

The meeting started at nine. After introductions around the room, Lew had the two agents, Steve Briscoe and Brian Pokorny, lay out their plan, which included surveillance of the Brinkerhoff property until they had the signal from their head office in New York City to move in and arrest Mathew Brinkerhoff.

The agents said that the coordinating investigators at the head office had made contact with Alex Brinkerhoff and would be meeting with her and her lawyer later in the day for more details on how her ex-husband was embezzling from his investors and laundering money using his art collection. She had been told to bring documents they could use to get a warrant. Until then, the agents on-site had been told to stand by and keep watch on the property.

"That's all good," said Lew, when they had finished. "But we have an individual, Sarah Hatch, whom some of us feel may be at risk of bodily harm so long as she is in the Brinkerhoff home. If Matt discovers she is one of the informants . . ."

"I understand," said Steve, the older of the two agents. "We are concerned too, but we can't get her out of there before arresting the suspect. If he gets wind that we're closing in, he could run. We're too close to Canada, and we know he has access to a private plane. We can't risk his fleeing the country."

"I have an idea how we can get Sarah out of danger," said Judith, standing up so everyone could hear her better. "Why don't I pretend that I'm the director of the Arts Center in Rhinelander and I have just stopped by the house hoping to catch Mr. Brinkerhoff while he's visiting to see if we might hold a fund raiser where people could view his collection. I'll bet you anything he won't answer his door, but Sarah Hatch may."

"I could text her to watch for you," said Mallory from the back of the room, where she was standing next to Osborne. She would probably answer it anyway, because

Matt is in a meeting today with two investors from Minneapolis."

"Partners in the money laundering operation?" asked Steve.

"I don't think so," said Mallory. "Sarah said he's been courting new investors for his hedge fund all along this month and meeting with them at his place on Hemlock Lake. She thinks he set this meeting up as a cover for moving the art, because it gives him a reason to be up north and close to the border."

"Excuse me, Sheriff Ferris," said Brian, the other agent, "but this woman's idea doesn't work. You can't just knock on the man's door out of the blue."

"Why not?" asked Judith. "I'll say I saw his black Range Rover go by my summer cottage, so I hoped I could catch him at home and put a bug in his ear. I'll be very ingratiating and let him assume I'm some well-meaning art patron who has no sense of how valuable his time is. Look at me, do I look dangerous? I'm a sixty-five-year-old woman who, for all he knows, spends her time walking her dog, feeding her cats, and baking cookies for her grandbabies. None of that is true. I don't own a dog, but I can make it look good."

Lew studied her as she spoke. Judith was not a beautiful woman, certainly not the type who applied full face makeup daily, had her hair colored monthly, and wore close-fitting pants more appropriate for women in their thirties. She was not unattractive either.

She was plain in her appearance. Her wavy midlength gray hair was tucked behind her ears, which were pierced to hold simple black studs. The only makeup she wore was a light application of a pale-red lipstick. Her cheeks were full under watchful dark eyes, and Lew could see she must have suffered acne as a teenager.

It would not be a challenge for Judith Hanson to play the role of a middle-aged busybody given to "dropping in" on her neighbors without warning.

"That's not a bad idea," said Osborne from the back of the room where he was standing with his arms crossed, listening. "You don't live here, Brian. This isn't the big city. We drop in on our neighbors all the time."

As he spoke, Osborne thought of Ray, who had a bad habit of "popping in" for a Saturday morning cup of coffee at some rather awkward times. Awkward now that Lew often stayed over and they had discovered pleasant, private ways to enjoy their weekend mornings.

"But how can you be sure you can get to this Sarah person?" asked one of the deputies.

"Well, if she doesn't answer the door, I'll keep chatting away, and I'll bet you anything he'll shove me off on her as soon as he can. Then I'll figure out a way to get her out of there."

"But that puts you at risk," said Lew.

"I've got a gun."

Silence in the room.

"What?" asked Brian, the younger of the two agents, sounding stupefied.

"I hunt," said Judith, "birds. I'm a good shot."

"I don't think you can walk into that house carrying a twelve-gauge shotgun," said Brian.

"Twenty-gauge, over and under," corrected Judith. "Made in Japan. Inherited it from my father. But that's not the gun I'll have, of course. I have a concealed-carry permit for a Smith & Wesson 357."

"What on earth?" It was Lew's turn to be astounded.

"Before I retired and moved back here, I was head of production for a large printing company over in the Fox Valley," said Judith. "I had many meetings with one of our major suppliers whose headquarters were in a rough neighborhood in Milwaukee. I needed protection, but fact is, I never had to use it."

She paused a moment, maybe to give the others time to digest this new information, then went on.

"Here's a plan that I think might work," said Judith. "I get Sarah Hatch into a conversation about a fund-raising event, even though I imagine she's feeling pretty shaky right now. Correct?" Judith caught Mallory's eye, and she nodded, confirming her supposition.

"After I sling some BS about the Arts Center, I'll ask her to walk me to my car so I can give her my business card and a brochure on our organization. Then she jumps in and I speed off with her beside me. He'll assume we're still talking about a fund raiser . . ."

"The businessmen from Minneapolis are there now, so Matt's not likely to be too worried about Sarah," Mallory said. "Not at first, anyway."

"And we'll be guarding the driveway and the county road in both directions," said one of the deputies.

"Sound too easy?" asked Lew, gazing around the room.

"Simple works best," said Osborne.

"Good point," said Lew. She saw the hesitation in the agents' eyes, but she also saw determination on Judith's face. For the first time, it occurred to her to wonder if Judith had taken the position as Dani's admin in order to be close to law enforcement records so she could research her sister's death.

"Let me think this over," said Lew, nodding to the agents.

She pulled them out of the conference room and into her office.

*   *   *

"I like what Judith Hansen is suggesting," said Lew.

"No," said Steve, "we can't risk this Brinkerhoff getting the slightest whiff we're onto him. Absolutely can't happen."

"I understand," said Lew. "All right, I'll let my people know. Are you comfortable in that small office where we've set you up?"

"It works," said Brian. "If you're okay with where things are right now, Steve and I are going to run and grab an early lunch." Lew nodded and left the room.

* * *

Back in the conference room with everyone who had been waiting on her decision with the two agents, Lew reported their concern.

"I couldn't disagree more," said Mallory, getting to her feet and waving her arms. "They get to be 'careful' while I get a dear friend killed? Are you kidding me? Sarah is so close to losing it—I know she's terrified. We have got to get her out of there."

Lew surveyed the room. "Judith?" she asked, "how soon can you get going?"

Everyone in the room got to their feet, scrambling for the door. Lew waved toward Judith and the seven deputies in the room, saying, "Let's map out where everyone will be stationed while Judith goes in. She needs to know where you'll be. Dani, check with everyone's phones so you can set trackers that will tell us who is where."

"Got it," said Dani, jumping to her feet.

"Now, Judith," said Lew, stopping her as she was about to leave the room. "If this doesn't work, we do have more options. Do not put yourself or Sarah Hatch in danger. Understand?"

With a nod, Judith was gone.

Chapter
Thirty-One

Praying the security guards would let her in, Judith pulled up at the wrought iron gate guarding the Brinkerhoff estate. After pushing a button on the intercom, she waited a moment before leaning forward to say, "Hello, I'm Judith Hansen with the Arts Center of Rhinelander. I'm just stopping by to introduce myself and drop off a brochure and a proposal for Mr. Brinkerhoff. I don't have an appointment, but this shouldn't take more than a minute.

"Oh, and I'm sure hoping Mr. Brinkerhoff is at home, as I would love to meet him." She smiled her most gracious smile into what she was sure was a security camera aimed at her face.

No one answered, but after a long moment the gate swung open. Judith inhaled, steeling herself. She drove up the long drive past meticulously trimmed shrubs interspersed with young pines. As she neared the horizontal glass-walled house, she was struck by the setting.

Unlike many lake houses, which had wide lawns designed to emphasize their magnificence, this contemporary home had been shoehorned into a dense stand of pine trees, their branches crowding the flat roof. A flat roof? In snow country? Judith shook her head.

That wasn't the only surprise. She could see past the house to the lake. It was a lake view so close that the owner must have had an unusual variance allowing his builder to locate the house at such a short distance from the water. Most structures built in the Northwoods over the last fifty years had been required to be set back hundreds of feet from the shoreline. This couldn't be more than fifty feet.

Ah, thought Judith, *money talks.*

She pulled into one of three parking spots next to the walkway leading up to the entrance to the house. Hers was the not the only car parked there. A white SUV with Wisconsin plates was in one spot, a small sedan in the other. She assumed they might be rental cars, one driven by the investors in from Minneapolis, the other by Sarah Hatch. Off to the right was a larger parking area with two vans visible at the far end. Security? Or were they being used to transport the art to Canada?

She felt herself tense, acutely aware that she was arriving at a time and in a place where she had to take care to say the right things and make a move, as casually as possible, that could save a life. At the same time, she was determined to meet the man whose name was one of three people involved in her sister's death. She had to see his face.

As she turned off the ignition, she mentally calculated the length of the driveway. With a sense of relief, she decided it would be possible to speed out of there to the main road, where deputies were waiting, in less than two minutes.

She marched up the walkway to the entrance and reached to press an ivory bird's egg designed to pass as a doorbell. The door opened before she could touch the button.

"Sarah?" A petite woman in her midthirties, her curly black hair held back from her face with two burgundy-colored barrettes, greeted her with an attempt at a smile. Judith felt rather than saw the woman's body trembling as they shook hands.

"Yes, I'm Sarah Hatch, and Mr. Brinkerhoff is in a meeting," said Sarah, stepping back to beckon her inside the foyer. "You'll have to meet him another day, but let me take your information." She managed a weak smile. "I'm sure we can look it over later and get back to you soon."

"Oh, thank you," said Judith, pushing forward into the house. "It's a proposal for a fund raiser to be held next spring. Be wonderful if I could hear back in a week or so. These things take a good deal of planning, you know." She smiled her best false smile.

Sarah waved her hands, saying, "I'm not sure if we can manage a response in such a short time frame. Mr. Brinkerhoff is under a lot of pressure right now. Business matters, you know."

"I appreciate that," said Judith, peering over the woman's shoulder as she spoke. "O-o-oh, I can see a wonderful O'Keeffe on that wall behind you. And is that a Jasper Johns? Heavens! You have a Morris Louis here too."

Judith's command of contemporary artists and their work might be limited, but she did recognize these paintings thanks to a semester studying contemporary art history that she'd taken in college years ago.

She pushed past Sarah to get a good look around the room. Her goal was to convince whoever might be watching that she was an overenthusiastic art patron thrilled to be in the billionaire's mansion. She was hurriedly scanning the walls of the elegant room when she saw a workman enter and, with gloved hands, take down the Georgia O'Keeffe painting.

Sarah, looking nonplussed, tugged at Judith's sleeve. "Yes, it's a stunning collection, but I've not had time to discuss your fund raiser with Mr. Brinkerhoff yet. May I have your brochure?" she said in an urgent tone. "You mention a proposal. Is there something on paper you can leave with us?"

"Yes, of course," said Judith, backing toward the front entrance as she fumbled in her purse. "Oh . . . wait, darn.

Oh, gosh, Ms. Hatch, I must have left it on the seat of my car. Walk down to the car with me, if you don't mind. I'll hand it over and not take any more of your time."

"Excuse me, Sarah," said a tall, blond-haired man walked into the hallway just as Sarah and Judith were moving toward the front door. "I need you in this meeting." He reached out and grabbed Sarah's arm.

"Oh, Mr. Brinkerhoff, I'd love to meet—"

"I'll be there in a minute," said Sarah, interrupting Judith while trying to pull away from Matt. Judith waited by the door, which she had opened. She watched the man who was grasping Sarah's arm so tightly that she winced as she tried to pull away.

"No, *now*," said the man. He looked at Judith, his eyes dark with irritation. Speaking dismissively, he gave a nod to Judith as he said, "Leave your papers in the box at the front gate as you leave. Sarah can look them over later. Good-bye." And he yanked Sarah out of the room. As Sarah was pulled around the corner of the foyer, she looked back at Judith, desperation in her eyes.

Defeated but determined, Judith walked slowly down to her car, thinking, *Lew was right. This seemed too easy.*

Backing out of her parking space, she took a long look back at the house. Again she was struck by the looming presence of the pine trees. As soon as she reached the county road, she pulled over to call Lew with the frustrating news.

"Let the deputies know you are okay and no one is in the car," said Lew. "Then hurry back here. Ray and I have an idea."

As she drove back to Loon Lake, she couldn't help but think of that last expression in Sarah's eyes. Had her sister looked like that in the minutes before her death?

* * *

Maggie and Judith had been closer than many sisters. With both their parents working full-time, they had been true latchkey kids and happy to make their time together relaxing and fun. Because Maggie was eight years older, she was put in charge of her little sister.

Together they would pore over their mother's cook-books and plan out desserts to make together. Their mother, thrilled to not have that burden, would buy every item on their list of ingredients. Then the two sisters would get started. Maggie would split up their duties, making sure they took turns mixing and tasting the cookie batter or frosting or candy decorations that they used.

They rarely fought, and Judith's most fun times were watching her big sister try out makeup and clothes before going to the Friday night dances at the high school. When Maggie got invited to the prom her sophomore year, she let Judith hang out in her bedroom and watch while she and two girlfriends swooned over the pictures in magazines of prom dresses and hairstyles that the older girls might wear. Later they all got up and danced to Bruce Springsteen on Maggie's CD player, stopping to help Judith refine her moves. She had never felt so grown-up.

The summer she died, Maggie had shared with Judith some details of her secret crush, a boy she had met at a beer party one of her friends had hosted at the family cottage when her parents were out of town.

"I really like this one guy. He's taller than me; he's really cute, with this long blond hair that gets in his eyes. Oh, and Judith, he says he's a good tennis player. He asked me to play with him next Saturday when he gets a day off. See, he's one of the counselors here for the summer from Camp Ashwabagon. Really, really cute, Judith."

Maggie never had the chance to play tennis with the "cute blond guy." Was it Matt Brinkerhoff she was referring to? Or one of the other three boys? Would Phil Henman remember what color hair the three junior counselors had? Would he find it strange if she asked?

Chapter
Thirty-Two

Mallory and Osborne jumped up as Judith walked into Lew's office. "Don't feel bad, Judith," said Mallory. "Dad and Ray have an idea that Lew is sure will work to protect Sarah."

"Really?"

"We'll use Ray's new pontoon to watch from the water," said Lew. "That way we can be sure she's safe when the feds go in to arrest Matt Brinkerhoff. When we get the signal from Steve and Brian, I'll call and let her know we're right there for her. All she has to do is walk down to the dock, where we'll be waiting. Matt won't be able to stop her."

*   *   *

Ray's pontoon was one of the largest pontoons ever seen on the Loon Lake chain. Helping to produce a documentary on muskie fishing for Netflix had paid well and gotten him plenty of free publicity for his guiding business.

However, he had promised to provide a large pontoon for the project—and that had cost him nearly every penny he'd been paid. He didn't mind. What was life for if not investing in the equipment that made it possible to be the best, most sought-after muskie fishing guide ever?

The good news had been that he had enough money left over from that purchase to pay the property tax on his trailer home.

Back in her office, Lew laid out the new plan: she, Ray, and Officer Todd Donovan from her Loon Lake Police Department would provide surveillance of the Brinkerhoff property from the water using Ray's pontoon.

"Ray's pontoon has a larger motor than the one used by the sheriff's department," she said, "and with Ray and Todd Donovan on board, we'll be prepared if he tries to leave by boat or one of those Cessna seaplanes that I hear he uses."

She saw the stricken look on Mallory's face and said, "I'm sorry, Mallory, but the pontoon can hold only so many people. You know that, right?"

After working out the timing to meet up with Ray, Lew excused everyone from her office. Mallory followed Judith down the hall to her cubicle in Dani's office. "Judith," said Mallory, with tears in her eyes, "I hate this.

They won't let me on the pontoon, and I have to be there. *I have to be there for my friend.*"

Judith put her arm across Mallory's shoulders and squeezed. "I know. I want to be there too. For my sister. Let me think this through, okay?"

Chapter
Thirty-Three

Sarah picked at her food while having lunch with Matt and the two men from Minneapolis. They were all happy, celebrating Matt's financial analysis showing the increased value of their investment in his hedge fund. The satisfaction on Matt's face made her feel sick to her stomach. How many days would it be before the two investors learned the truth, that they had lost thousands of dollars after trusting brilliant Matthew Brinkerhoff?

After the two men had driven off in their rental car and Matt had left the dining room for his office, Sarah walked through the kitchen to the rear entrance to the house. She found half a dozen paintings lined up near the door to the large four-car garage. She wasn't surprised, as she, like Judith, had seen the workman pull the O'Keeffe off the wall.

The lack of care for the priceless objects about to be loaded into a van made her shiver. Making up her mind to salvage a few of the treasures that she could handle herself, she raced back to the guest wing and grabbed the keys to her rental car. Moving down the hall past Matt's office, she saw his door was closed. She knew that even though his office looked out over the parking area, he had a habit of keeping the curtains drawn against the strong afternoon sun. Thank goodness. She would have time to get to her car unseen.

She hurried back to where the paintings were stacked and was relieved to see that none had been moved. Moving fast, she grabbed the O'Keeffe and two other small artworks, letting herself through the door to the garage and the one open garage door. It was a quick walk to her rental car, where the trunk opened without a sound, and she slipped the paintings in, setting them face-to-face on top of each other, hoping they wouldn't get damaged. One was small enough she could tuck it alongside the other two.

She stepped back and closed the trunk. As she walked over to the main walkway, she glanced up at the windowed walls, behind which were the dining room and Matt's office. Did she see the curtain pull back a few inches? That had to be her imagination.

The morning had gone pretty well. She had not let on that she knew Matt was about to have the most priceless paintings moved out of the house over the next day or two; she had not let on that she knew he had already embezzled millions of dollars from the hedge fund. She suspected the payments he had contracted to make to the auction houses from which she had secured the artworks would soon be voided. For the moment, she tried not to think of the consequences his actions would have on her business. Right now, she had to save herself and what she could of the art.

Her suitcase was packed. She hurried back down the hall to the guest wing to get it. Next stop was Dr. Paul Osborne's house, where she could be safe until her flight that evening out of Rhinelander.

Once in her room, her cell phone rang. She shut the door fast.

"Sarah? This is Dani Wright in Sheriff Ferris' office. I have a quick question for you. Do you have a minute?"

"Yes, but I have to keep my voice low," said Sarah. "Sound travels in this place. What do you need? And please tell my friend, Mallory, if you can that I'm going to her father's house, leaving right now—"

"Yes, I'll do that. Sarah, do you have an iPhone? Mallory told me you do."

"Yes, why?"

"Sheriff Ferris asked me to set trackers for every person participating involved in the surveillance and investigation of Mr. Brinkerhoff. The federal agents are here and waiting for signal from their head office to move in. I need to track where everyone is located in case . . . um . . . anything changes.

"I can do that without your cooperation, but if you will check your phone so it will allow 'friends' to track your phone, I'll be able to get more accurate location data. I'm working to get this set up for all our deputies, even your friend and her father. We need to know everyone's location."

"Done," said Sarah in a whisper. "I had it on already. Mallory knows that."

"We wanted to be sure. One more question—do you have the personal cell phone number for Matt Brinkerhoff?"

"No, just the one for his office, but he has a personal assistant who checks it regularly for him."

"Damn," said Dani. "Oh well. Bye."

Sarah grabbed her suitcase and opened the bedroom door. A loud voice stopped her.

"Alex, are you crazy?" Matt was shouting into the phone in his office, but the closed door did little to keep the volume down. "You told who what? You told Sarah Hatch *that*?" The fury in his voice was stunning.

Sarah closed the door as softly as possible even as her hands were shaking. She had waited too long.

She had no doubt what would happen next. After locking the bedroom door, she ran to the sliding door that opened onto the small balcony outside her room. She slid it open, grabbed her suitcase and purse, shoved her cell phone in the back pocket of her pants, and stepped out onto the balcony. Closing the door behind her, she headed down the narrow metal stairs, hoping she could get through the bushes surrounding the house and make it to her car.

Before she got to the bottom of the stairs, she heard the sliding door above her open.

Chapter Thirty-Four

～

Judith had pulled her chair up to Dani's desk so they could both see the wide-screen monitor on her desk as they added the trackers for Lew, Ray, Officer Donovan, and each of the deputies. Judith made the calls, and Dani added the data and watched as each location popped up on her screen.

"We should put Mallory and Doc Osborne in too," said Judith. "Do you think it would be okay if Mallory sat here with us? I know she's a wreck, and it might help if she can see that Sarah is safe."

"Fine with me," said Dani, "but I would check with Sheriff Ferris to be sure."

Judith hurried down to Lew's office. "Is it okay for Mallory to be in Dani's office with us?"

"Of course," said Lew, "I know she's worried sick. Please check with Doc Osborne and let him know the feds haven't made a move yet. He's hoping Sarah Hatch will get to his place safe and sound. Does Dani have a tracker on Matt Brinkerhoff yet?"

"I'll check. I know she's working on it."

Lew reached for her phone to check in with Steve and Brian. "Any news from your team in New York? We're ready with our backup when you are."

"Nothing yet," said Steve, "but I expect to hear any-time. Where are you, Sheriff Ferris?"

"My office, but on my way out the door to the Brinker-hoffs'. When you get there, you'll see a pontoon anchored a short distance off from the Brinkerhoff docks. That will be me with two of my people. One of my deputies will be working a spinning rod, so anyone watching will think we're just a couple of fishermen.

"But Steve, listen. Immediately after you arrest Brinkerhoff, please tell the woman, Sarah Hatch, to meet us down at the docks. She's under a lot of stress right now, and she'll need some emotional support fast. Don't forget she'll be one of the government's best witnesses too."

"Will do. We'll take good care of her, Sheriff."

Off the phone, Lew headed for the door. She knew Ray had to be waiting at the landing with his pontoon ready.

Chapter
Thirty-Five

Frantic at the sound of footsteps, Sarah pushed her suitcase to one side, tipping it over. After grabbing her car keys and cell phone, she threw the purse down and ran, shoving the keys in one pocket, keeping her phone in her hand as she edged her way along a narrow strip of grassy dirt that lay between the house and an incline ending in a pile of rocks and boulders. Late-afternoon shadows made the terrain difficult to see. If only she could get around the house, she knew she could reach the car.

Tripping, she slipped and slid down into the rocks. Getting to her feet, she plunged ahead. Her right foot sank into a hole between two boulders even as her momentum carried her forward. Down she went, her right leg between her ankle and knee bending the wrong way. Stifling a scream with her fist, she lost her grasp on her phone. The phone flew into the air, disappearing as she grabbed for a boulder to steady herself.

Sarah felt herself slip down into a hollow between two large boulders. Footsteps were pounding down the stairs from the balcony. She forced herself further into the crevasse between the boulders, It was too dark in the rock pit for her to see if her body was hidden or not. She held her breath. Hot blades of pain shooting through her leg made her want to cry out. She pressed her face hard against the rock, praying she couldn't be seen in the deepening shadows.

Footsteps got closer, and she waited. They kept going in the direction of the tall pines guarding the house, a logical direction for her to have gone—the direction she'd been trying to go before falling.

She let out a breath. He hadn't seen her. But he would be back. She raised her head—she had to find her phone. But then her vision started going black, and she passed out.

Chapter
Thirty-Six

～

Dani and Judith watched the monitor as the trackers for Lew's deputies showed they had taken their positions along the town road as instructed. They could see the federal agents waiting in their vehicle nearby. Sarah's tracker appeared close to the location Dani had marked as the site of the Brinkerhoff house. It did not appear to be moving.

"Why no movement?" asked Mallory, who had joined Dani and Judith in the office. "Oh, I'll bet she's waiting in her room for the agents to arrive."

"Very likely," said Dani. "There's a margin of error in these location markers."

Mallory and Osborne had pulled in extra chairs to be near but not in the way of Dani's screen. No one spoke as they waited. "This is taking forever," said Mallory with a sigh. Osborne could see the anxiety building in her eyes.

"Settle down, Mal," he said, "Lew has this under control."

Every few minutes, Dani would check her emails. It was her responsibility to keep track of any situations occurring throughout the county, whether lost dogs or runaway teens. She was hoping nothing unrelated to the current crisis would show up. During this check, one did come in. It was from the Wausau Crime Lab. Keeping one eye on the monitor with the location markers, she decided to read the new email.

"Oh, this is interesting," she said, urging Judith to take a look too.

The email was from Bruce Peters. The microbiologist who had been searching for a lab that could pull DNA from Dr. Roger Nystrom's microscopic slides of forensic evidence collected during rape examinations years ago had finally found a lab that could do the work. Lew had given Bruce the green light to have the slides analyzed, and he had gotten the results a short time ago.

Dani's phone rang. It was Bruce Peters. "Dani, did my email and the attachment arrive safely?" he asked.

"It sure did," she said. "Lew isn't here right now, but she'll be pleased."

"She's pleased? I'm the one who's pleased," he said with a chortle. "She promised me a day in the trout stream if this worked. When she gets in, tell her to check her calendar. And let me know if you get a match on that, will you please?"

"You bet," said Dani. "I'm on a deadline right now, though. I'll run it through our databases later." She hung up.

Turning to Judith, she said, "I just received the DNA sample from the autopsy records of your sister's death. That was in the late sixties, right?"

Judith nodded. She looked over at Doc, who was sitting nearby. "Did you hear what Dani just said? Bruce Peters sent a DNA sample that has been recovered from those microscopic files you said you found at the Wausau Crime Lab. Would that be from the file that had my sister's name on it?"

"I wasn't sure that could happen," said Osborne. "Dani, is it too much trouble to ask you to do a DNA search now? Maybe we should wait . . ."

After a moment's thought, Dani said, "I'll give it a try. Only takes a few keystrokes. And if it doesn't happen right away, then we'll go for it tomorrow. I'll be surprised if it does work. Right now all we're doing is waiting on Steve and Brian, so let's give it a try while we wait." She smiled at Judith. "I know you've been waiting a long time for this."

"How is it, really?" asked Judith. Anxious as she was to see if there would be any DNA match to the slides kept for so many years by the forensic pathologist, she didn't think it wise to jeopardize the federal agents' efforts to arrest Matt Brinkerhoff.

Dani shrugged. "Not sure, but Sheriff Ferris told me that when it came in, go ahead. The McBride County Sheriff's Department is authorized to access any of the national genealogy sites we might need, so let's do it. I can always stop."

Dani's fingers moved fast over her keyboard. The first break occurred when she entered the sample in the GEDmatch research database. "This is a national database that contains data from several of the more popular ancestry tests used by people tracing their family trees, like 23andMe, Ancestry/DNA, FamilyTreeDNA, and My Heritage.

"You've probably heard of all those," she said, looking up at the three people crowding around her. "Those are ones everyone uses. GEDmatch is the best. It allows people to search tests from all those sources as long as an individual has given permission to allow the searches, including those by law enforcement like us. Most people do give permission, which helps me." Her fingers kept dancing.

When Dani's search quickly found a match to the DNA sample Bruce had sent, she was surprised. "I have a hit," she said simply, deciding not to say more until the match could be confirmed, which would require one more database search.

"How does that happen so easily?" asked Osborne. "I expected this to take days, and you're being nice trying to take our minds off Sarah Hatch for a few minutes."

"No, Doc," said Dani, "so many people are doing family searches these days that I'm sure someone's wife or mother submitted her DNA sample in order to find more details on her family history. I did it and got great stuff on my grandfather and great-grandfather on my dad's side.

"Now, since the original DNA sample was connected to a criminal case"—she gave Judith an apologetic look as she spoke—"we'll put the information I now have into our law enforcement database." Again the fingers moved swiftly. To her surprise, she got an immediate hit.

"Oh gosh," she said, alarmed by the information.

"What?" Judith leaned over her shoulder.

The DNA match was to *Matthew Brinkerhoff*. And it was a full match, not a partial one, indicating a relative.

"How can that be?" asked Dani. "I'll bet it's really a partial match to the kid, Barry—he's the one whose DNA is in the database."

Judith waited, holding her breath.

Dani studied the current law enforcement file connected to the sample. "Oh, wait, Matthew Brinkerhoff's DNA is here, from a misdemeanor three years ago." She read on. Matthew and two friends had been drinking at a local bar to the point that the bartender that night, concerned when they turned down his offer to call them a taxi for their drive home, alerted the sheriff's department. The bartender had not wanted his business or himself to be held liable for a drunk-driving accident.

A sheriff's deputy watching a back road popular with late-night drivers on their way to summer homes on Hemlock Lake spotted the swerving SUV. It was being driven by the overserved host of the boys' night out: Matthew Brinkerhoff.

The deputy pulled the car over. He charged Brinkerhoff with a DUI, which led to the misdemeanor charge. The driver was required to provide a DNA sample, and so, even though his lawyer later got the DUI charge dismissed, his DNA sample remained in the database.

"No question about it, that DNA sample from 1967 is a match to Matthew Brinkerhoff," said Dani. "What was I thinking? Of course it couldn't be his son—this is from 1967. I have to let Lew know ASAP." She reached for her phone and called Lew's cell.

"Dani here. Something just happened that you should know, if it's okay to talk."

"Go ahead. I'm just parking at the boat landing at Hemlock Lake. I've heard nothing from Steve and Brian. Have you?"

"No. And Bruce Peters sent us the DNA sample from the autopsy report on Judith's sister, the one who was killed years ago. I hope you don't mind—since we're sitting here waiting, I went ahead and ran a search. Got a match right away, and it's to *Matt* Brinkerhoff."

"You must mean a partial match—to his son, Barry. We've got his DNA, not his father's," said Lew.

"We have Matt's too," said Dani, "from a DUI a couple years ago. He was never charged, but his DNA is in the law enforcement database."

"Does Judith know?"

"Yes, she's sitting here. We all are. Doc Osborne and Mallory are here too."

Lew was silent for a long moment, then she asked, "Dani, do we have a tracker on Matt Brinkerhoff?"

"Oh, darn, no," said Dani. "I was going to try GPS to find him, because we don't have a personal cell number—"

"Call the kid at his mother's home right now. The boy will have his father's number. We should have had that already. The file on Barry Brinkerhoff's arraignment is on my desk. The mother's name and number will be right at the top. While you do that, I'll put a call in to Judge Perriman's office and get a warrant so we can track that guy's phone. Be sure to text me the number when you get it."

Before calling the judge, Lew realized she needed not one but two warrants regarding Matthew Brinkerhoff: one to be able to track his cell phone number, and another for his arrest on suspicion of sexual assault resulting in the death of Margaret Hanson, age sixteen.

Dani put the phone down and ran down the hall to Lew's office. She found the file, opened it, and placed a call to the former Mrs. Brinkerhoff. After a quick explanation, she could hear the woman ask her son for his father's cell phone number.

She ran back to her office, sat down at the computer and put in the number for Matt Brinkerhoff's phone, and waited. A tracker came up, showing him at a distance from Sarah Hatch's tracker.

Mallory, who had been quiet and rigid with concern for her friend during Dani's work, spoke at last, her eyes on the tracker. "That's a relief," she said.

Chapter
Thirty-Seven

～

Lew met up with Ray and Officer Todd Donovan at the boat landing on Hemlock Lake. Ray had the outboard motors purring as the pontoon waited for the three of them to board.

"I find it hard to believe the length of this delay from the federal officials on the East Coast," said Lew. "I know Steve and Brian are standing by. They're parked up on County W with my deputies. Let's hope we get the green light shortly. I would have been here sooner, but I was told to expect a two-hour delay. That was an hour ago. Let's hope things happen soon.

"Something else you need to know. Dani Wright just ran a DNA search on a cold case DNA sample Bruce sent up from the crime lab. The sample was taken years ago from the body of a young teenager who was sexually assaulted, beaten, and left to die. The original DNA sample belongs to someone familiar to us today: Matthew Brinkerhoff. The one and only."

She climbed onto the pontoon and took a seat behind Ray's. Todd sat next to him. The sky overhead was calm, the clouds pillowy bands of blue gray. The water over which they were skimming gleamed with a metallic sheen as it rippled toward the private beaches dotting the shoreline.

Ray looked back at Lew as he drove, saying, "We're almost there. I did a test run this morning to be sure there wouldn't be any unmarked rock piles, which this lake is known for. Brinkerhoff's place is around that bend just past the old Ashwabagon Camp." He nudged Todd. "See the old summer camp sign? Maybe a quarter mile past that point."

The shoreline just beyond the wide beach area that had belonged to the summer camp was heavily forested, the tips of balsams indicating that the wooded area extended far back toward the town roads that gave people access to the area.

As they neared the Brinkerhoff property, Ray slowed the pontoon, and Lew raised her binoculars. She had a good view of the back of the house and the trees crowding around it. She was surprised to see how close the house was to the shoreline, especially at a time when regulations kept new construction at least two hundred feet away.

"Do you see that, Ray?" She leaned forward and kept her voice low, as she was well aware of how sound traveled over water. She did not need to alert Brinkerhoff or his security people to their approach. "That house is brand-new, and it is so close to the water. How much did Brinkerhoff have to pay to get past the county regs?"

"My hunch is that was where the old lodge was, the one his great-grandfather built back in the late 1880s. Bet he was able to use the original footprint to allow him to build so close."

As he was talking, Ray let the anchor drop so the pontoon would be stationary. He got out of the driver's seat and stood to one side of Lew. Picking up a spinning rod, which he had set down before starting out, he started to cast off the back of the pontoon, just as Lew had planned.

She was pleased. So far they looked like innocent fishermen, uninterested in anything on shore. Raising the binoculars again, she scanned the property. She made a mental note to research the location in an old copy of the county plat book.

Concentrating on the house, she could make out an odd addition high up on the back wall. It took her a minute to realize she was looking at a balcony.

"See that?" she asked Ray in a whisper.

"What? I see the house but no movement. Do you see something?" he asked as he cast. Todd had binoculars up and was watching the front of the house.

"Just that they built a balcony off the back of the house. Why do that on a glass house? And right into the trees."

Ray shook his head. "Who knows. I find it disturbing the place has a flat roof."

"Hey, guys," said Todd, leaning back with his voice low, "I see a van at the top of the drive. Looks like it's driving toward the county road. Should it be stopped?"

Lew checked her phone. "No signal from Steve and Brian yet," she said. "I'll let them handle it. They know that Brinkerhoff is planning to move the art to Canada. I told the agents to let their people in New York know that we're only an hour and a half from Lake Superior. A boat can reach Canada in a matter of hours. They've assured me they'll be watching air and boat traffic, so let's hope that's right."

Lew got a text from Steve. "Okay, Ray, Todd. I've just been told they got the go-ahead. Steve and Brian have been parked about fifteen minutes away, making sure Brinkerhoff's security couldn't pick up any of their signals. He should let us know when they've apprehended Brinkerhoff."

With one eye toward the docks fronting the Brinkerhoff beach area, Ray kept casting. Todd, meanwhile, was focused on the lakeside view of the house, where a wide stone stairway swept from the deck down to two docks, on which were moored a pontoon, two Jet Skis, and three motorboats.

The three people on the pontoon sat silent as the late afternoon sun dipped to the west. Above the house and off to the left, they could see the driveway that led to the county road. The place looked still: no visible movement behind the windowed walls.

*   *   *

Back at the station, Dani was watching the monitor, tracking the movements of the agents' cars as they approached the property. *Steve and Brian are less than five minutes away*, she texted Lew.

Lew tensed, worried that Matt Brinkerhoff, faced with arrest, might try something extreme. She wouldn't put it past him to try to hold Sarah Hatch hostage. Under extreme stress, people had been known to act irrationally.

The agents' car appeared at the top of the driveway.

Chapter
Thirty-Eight

⁓

Sarah came to and struggled up on her elbows. Rolling onto one side, she reached down to touch her pant leg where it covered her shin. She felt a soft edge of bone protruding far enough that she knew it was broken. The pant leg was dry, so she knew it hadn't broken through the skin, or she'd be a bloody mess.

With a sigh, she tipped her head back against the rock and tried to figure out what to do. Her phone. If she could find her phone, she might be able to call for help. She wasn't sure. Several times while staying at the Brinkerhoffs', she had found that cell service was so spotty that calls and texts didn't go through. She had to try.

Pulling herself up on her good leg, she moved slowly in the direction where she thought her phone had landed. She ran her hands over the rocks and pebbles, but no luck. The sun was so low that it was dark among the rocks. Moving her hands over the rocky surface as she went, she kept pulling herself forward. Still no luck. She realized she had neared the edge of the rocky pile. She could see a narrow path leading into the nearby brush. A path? Who used a path out here?

Then she remembered a conversation about the hundreds of deer trails crossing the property. The security guards were concerned people might park on one of the logging roads and use a deer trail to get close to the house, close enough to break in. If the deer trails ran from the road to the house, then she could follow the trail back to the road.

Sarah was determined to keep hidden from Matt. Now that he knew Alex had alerted her to his plans to get out of the country with the art, who knew what he was capable of. For all she knew, she could be killed and her body left in the forest for the wolves and other animals to eat. Even if she was found, it would be too late—for her, for her family.

She couldn't go back to the house. He was sure to return there once he hadn't found her. She might be out here with a broken leg and no phone, but she was alive. She was alive, and she would stay alive.

Sarah gave up on the phone and started down the trail on her hands and one knee, keeping her broken leg extended behind her. Every few minutes, she pressed back tears of pain. She was under the pines trees now; every once in a while a branch would snag her hair. She kept going.

She was growing exhausted when she remembered she was wearing her new Apple watch. She checked it and tapped on it, then cursed herself for not learning more about the icons and how to use it. She didn't see an icon for making a phone call—or if there was one, she didn't recognize it. She tried hitting a couple of the images, but her only success was opening one that encouraged her to run or walk. *Sure, thank you.*

Sarah sank down on the trail, her body stretched out and her head in her hands. She was desperate for a rest. An owl hooted; an animal of some kind chattered away. What she did not hear was the sound of heavy footsteps. She let her eyes close.

Chapter
Thirty-Nine

Lew watched and waited, Ray and Todd close beside her. The two agents could be seen standing at the entrance to the house. Then they were inside. Minutes went by until Steve came running out of the house and down the stone walkway to the deck.

"Sheriff Ferris," he shouted, "no one is here."

Before she could say a word, Ray turned the ignition, the outboard motors roared, and the pontoon charged forward. Within seconds it was hydroplaning as it sped toward shore. He had the pontoon at the dock by the time Steve had reached it.

As Ray maneuvered the pontoon alongside the mooring, Lew jumped onto the dock where Steve was standing. "No one here," he said. "Did you see them leave? Did they take a boat?"

"No," said Lew, "they *have* to be here. Both Brinkerhoff and the Hatch woman. No way they've left. We would've seen them. Get back to the house," said Lew, running past him. "He has to be hiding in there somewhere. Check the garage. Is there a back way? Where's his security guys? They'll know."

"We just talked to the security guy on duty today," said Steve, breathing hard as he ran up the stairs behind her. "He said the only people leaving were two plumbers from Haas Plumbing, a local firm. Brinkerhoff had a meeting in the morning, but those people left right around noon. No one has come or gone since except the plumbers' van. The security guy said they come and go all the time because this place always has plumbing issues. He didn't think to check inside it. Could be Matt and the woman were hidden in the van?"

Lew stared at him. She looked over at Todd and said, "Officer Donovan, please put out an APB on that van. The deputies up on the county road must have seen it. Let's hope someone wrote down the license number."

Lew called Dani. "Dani, Steve and Brian said they can't find anyone here at the house. What do you see on the trackers? Matt?"

"He's near the house but moving away. I tried texting and calling you ten minutes ago, but—"

"We were on the pontoon. It was loud taking off, and—my fault—I wasn't paying attention," said Lew. "Tell me more. Give me an idea of the direction the tracker is going."

"Yes . . . it shows him moving away from the house." As Dani kept talking, Lew motioned to Ray and Todd.

"Very odd. Dani said it looks like the tracker for Matt is moving to the north and slightly to the west. The tracker for Sarah Hatch has shown no movement for over an hour. She has to be close."

"He's running through those pines," said Ray. "Got a few miles to go if he thinks he's getting out of here. Tough terrain in there."

Steve's partner, Brian, walked out of the house and hurried down to catch up with them. "News just in from New York. We got the arrest warrant, but they found out that the ex-wife, the one who turned him in? She called the guy to gloat. Over an hour ago. Dammit, she called before we had the go-ahead. He knows we're after him. What do we do now?"

Lew stared at him, stupefied. She wanted to say, *You and Steve are the experts who made us sit out here and wait. Kind of late to ask me for advice, isn't it?* But she kept her mouth shut.

Brian interrupted to say, "I checked the bedroom wing, and there's a balcony that runs the length of the three bedrooms back there. That's how they got out, I'll bet you."

"Okay, you two," said Lew to Brian and Steve, "you've met Ray Pradt." She nodded in Ray's direction. "What you don't know, and one reason he is a valuable asset to my department, is that he's a superb tracker—as good as a K-9 team, even better. If anyone can find someone running through these woods, he can."

"She's right," said Todd, "If Brinkerhoff thinks he's able to elude us, Ray's our best bet."

"Before we go, let's make sure everyone has a location tracker on their cell phone," said Lew, holding up her own. "On the off chance we get separated, I don't want anyone getting lost. Between Hemlock Lake and the Pelican River, there's a hell of a lot of forested land. The lake may be overbuilt, but not these woods."

She turned to leave, then stopped. "Hey, did you hear me?" Lew asked in a demanding tone of the two agents who had walked off from the group and were huddling together.

"Wait," said Steve, holding up one hand with his phone in the other, "I'm calling for air support. We need helicopters. Last thing we want is Matthew Brinkerhoff finding his way to Canada."

"Not sure the pilots can see through all that thick cover," said Lew. "Listen, everyone," she said, ignoring Steve, "Brinkerhoff has a good thirty minutes on us. The only chance we have to catch the guy is to move *right now. We've got to get going.*"

She started forward, then stopped, thinking.

"Officer Donovan," she said, pointing at Todd, "you stay here with Steve and Brian. Keep me posted on what they decide. We all need to know who is where and when. Confusion does not work."

She leaned close to Todd, saying in a low tone, "Those two are loose cannons. Don't hesitate to give them directions if you see they need it. Helicopters? Might work, but it's awful easy to hide in a pine forest like this." With that, she walked away from Todd and the two investigators, both of whom remained hunched over, glued to their phones.

She set off behind Ray as he moved slowly in the direction of the forest. "Careful," he called out as he held a branch of pine needles up high until Lew could duck under it. "Watch out for these branches. They can scratch a cornea."

Once around the house, the two of them pushed through a wall of arborvitae and stopped to look up. A narrow balcony with a wrought iron banister extended overhead. The ground close to the house was level for about three feet before dropping away at a steep pitch. A narrow stairway led down from the far end of the balcony.

Lew followed Ray over to the bottom of the stairs, where he needed only a moment before moving through the shrubs. Moving slowly, they slid down the embankment toward a wall of pine trees. Grabbing at branches and clumps of grass, Lew managed to keep herself from falling.

Ray had not gone far when he put a hand out to stop her. "Someone has been through here very recently. I got footprints—two sets . . . One goes in that direction." He pointed to the woods, then toward a large rock pile. "The smaller prints head that way." Lew walked in the direction of the rock pile. It was a scattering of boulders, smaller rocks and pebbles, leftovers from the glacier that had carved out the lakes of northern Wisconsin.

"Sarah Hatch. Has to be Sarah," said Lew. She watched as Ray walked through the boulders and rocks. He studied the dirt around the larger rocks, following them to a deer trail that led off to the east of where they were standing. "Someone dragged something through here . . . or they're crawling."

Lew, walking through a mound of grass near the edge of the rocks, saw something glinting in the softening sunlight. She reached down and found a cell phone. "Ray, stop," she said. "I got something." She held up the phone. "An iPhone. Has to be Sarah's."

"Can you try it?" asked Ray.

"I did. It's locked. Damn."

"Call Dani. She'll know how to make it work."

"No, I'll call Mallory and have her try calling Sarah. That way I'll know for sure." Lew reached for her cell and reached Dani. "Hey," she said, "I think I found Sarah Hatch's phone. Is Mallory right there? Ask her to call Sarah, and we'll see if I'm right."

Dani called over to Mallory, who was sitting across the room. "Lew wants you to try calling Sarah. She thinks she's got her phone. That would explain why her tracker hasn't been moving."

Mallory punched in the number and waited, and the phone in Lew's hand rang. A good sign. Lew felt heartened. They were on the right track.

Ray, who had not stopped while she was calling, walked swiftly along the deer trail. Sarah had managed to pull herself a good third of a mile through the brush and low-hanging branches.

Chapter Forty

Sarah, dragging herself along, heard feet approaching and panicked, assuming that Matt had tracked her down. Numb with fear, she closed her eyes and waited.

A soft male voice said, "Sarah? Sarah?"

It didn't sound like Matt. She opened her eyes and rolled over to look up. It wasn't anyone she knew, but he sounded friendly, and he was accompanied by a woman. She focused in on the woman, who looked familiar, and then realized it was Lew, her friend Mallory's almost-stepmother.

Lew and Ray helped Sarah sit up. They could see her broken leg.

"Where's Matt?" were her first words to Lew. "He's after me . . . isn't he?"

"We don't know where he is yet," said Lew, rubbing Sarah's back. "I imagine he thinks you ran into the forest. That's why our friend Ray here sees his tracks going in that direction."

"Now that you're okay, we're after him," said Ray, one arm supporting her. "I don't think you should walk, even if you could." He had palpated her right leg and felt the where the bone had broken. "With Sheriff Ferris' help, I can carry you on my back, if you're okay with that."

Sarah agreed, and Lew helped hoist her onto Ray's back. Sarah held tight around his shoulders as the three of them found their way slowly and carefully down the narrow path. As they walked, Sarah told them how she had heard Matt shouting into his phone at Alex.

"I am sure she couldn't wait to tell him she had turned him in to the feds, but why couldn't she have waited until he was arrested? She put me in danger. I could hear the fury in his voice.

"I should never have made this trip, but I was hoping to get a couple of those priceless paintings out of that house so I could save my gallery. It's all my family and I have. Now? Who knows what happens now?" Sarah's voice cracked.

Trying to reassure her, Lew said, "We'll find him. He can't have gone far."

"He was after me. I heard him. That's when I ran, but I fell. That's when I hurt myself so bad."

"Your fall was a blessing," said Lew.

"Sure was," echoed Ray. "He was after you so fast he never looked over in those rocks."

"I wish . . . I worry about the art. You know he had some men moving the art out of the house. It's worth a lot of money, like millions of dollars. Think anyone can stop that truck before it gets to Canada?"

"We're working on it," said Lew. "One of my deputies got the license number, and I put out an APB. The federal agents working with us to arrest Matt said they were told the van was supposed to meet a boat that had been chartered to get the art across Lake Superior to Canada. That's not going to happen."

"He sent other works of art to Canada already," said Sarah, "for shipping out of the country."

"The feds may be able to grab that too," said Lew. "Keep in mind, our government has relationships with the Canadian authorities when it comes to shipping goods illegally across international boundaries."

"I'll keep my fingers crossed," said Sarah, breathing a little easier in spite of the stabs of pain in her leg.

"You do that while we get you taken care of."

They had skirted the rock pile where Sarah had fallen and were close to steps leading up to the wide deck on the back of the house.

The ambulance was parked on the other side of the deck, waiting. As the EMTs loaded Sarah into the vehicle, Lew called Doc to let him know that he and Mallory could meet Sarah at the emergency room at St. Mary's Hospital. "They should have her there within fifteen minutes. Sorry to sound rushed, but can you put Dani on the line, please?"

Dani picked up immediately. "Don't worry, Judith and I will be here all night till you get that guy."

"Do we have a tracker on Brinkerhoff right now? Where the hell is he? Where are Steve and Brian? Is Todd out here somewhere? I'm putting you on speaker so Ray can hear too."

"Okay," said Dani, taking a deep breath, "first let me say that we think Matt is lost. He got a ways into those woods, and he's been kind of going in circles . . ."

"I can believe that," said Ray, listening over Lew's shoulder. "That pine forest is a killer, even for experienced hunters. The moon won't be up for another half hour, and that makes it very difficult to see where you're going. Especially if you're not used to traversing a dense woods."

"You asked about Steve and Brian. They drove out to the airport, where they're meeting a helicopter crew. Todd said to tell you he was going along with them so he can update you when you're ready."

"Back to Matt Brinkerhoff," said Lew, glancing at Ray while she spoke. "What do you see exactly on that screen? We're going in after him." She looked at Ray, who nodded as she spoke. "But it'll help if we know some direction, something so my deputies can be standing by when we find him."

"Hold on. Judith wants talk to you," said Dani.

"Lew," said Judith, her voice loud over the phone, "I know the general area where he is. I used to hunt back in there with my dad. Ray probably knows this too, but there are two logging roads off County W. They haven't been used in years and can be hard to find.

"I'm just back in the office from driving over to my parents' house, and I got my dad's old plat book out. I thought it might show that section better than any new maps. I got a finger on an area that might work if I let the deputies know where to drive in . . ."

"Yeah, they can drive in, park, and then work through the woods towards us, towards Matt." Lew got a strong nod of approval from Ray.

"Great. Judith, tell Dani to alert the deputies. You tell them where to go—"

"No, that may be difficult. I have a better idea," said Judith. "I'll drive out to the intersection of W and K and have them follow me. I know I can find that logging road. Let's hope their cruisers can make it down the road, then they can fan out and head into the woods in your direction. Make sense?"

"Worth a try."

While she was talking, Ray had run down to where he had docked his pontoon. He grabbed a couple of items out of his gear chest and ran back up. He handed Lew a head lamp and strong torch. He had another set for himself.

"Ready?" Ray asked her. He turned, crossed the deck, and hurried toward the rear of the house, where he had seen Matt's footprints leading into the pine forest. Lew ran after him.

Chapter Forty-One

When Dani and Judith hadn't heard from Lew while she and Ray were carrying Sarah out of the woods, Judith had taken a break to drive to her parents' home and search for the old plat book. Everything she had been seeing of Matt Brinkerhoff's tracker had reminded her of the area. It wasn't that far from where her childhood friends had lived with the family horses. It was also close to where she had hunted birds with her father. During the long walk she had taken last Saturday, she had seen signs of the old logging lane.

A quick study of the map in the plat book told her she was right. She even saw the name *Brinkerhoff* marking the lots belonging to the family. Grabbing the map, she started to leave the house. Her .357 in its case was sitting on the counter in the kitchen. She had carried it in her purse when she'd thought she would be able to get Sarah into her car and away from Brinkerhoff earlier.

Now, rushing to her car to go guide the deputies to the logging road, it crossed her mind to stop and get the gun. But should she do that? She was going to be in the company of law enforcement professionals well equipped to find and arrest the man who'd killed her sister. She paused—if she was honest with herself, she knew why she wanted to get her gun. She knew what was in the back of her mind: *how satisfying it would be to put an end to the man who was responsible for her sister's death and the death of her happy childhood.*

The second she let that thought into her head, she had another: a memory of Evan and Lily, her grandchildren, smiling at her through Facebook. They wanted a grandmother who lived near enough to them to be a part of their lives; they didn't need a grandmother in prison for exacting revenge. She shoved any thought of her gun out of her mind, turned the ignition in her car, and drove east out of town.

* * *

For Lew and Ray, it was slow going, as they encountered roots and dead tree limbs twenty or thirty feet long, some still green and heavy, others old and rotten. Eye-level branches on young pines threatened their faces as they struggled through.

"May take us an hour more to catch up with the razzbonya," said Ray, "but we'll get him. From everything I see, the man isn't trying to hide—he's lost, floundering."

"I want him floundering in prison," said Lew, tightening the band on her head lamp as she stayed close behind Ray.

*   *   *

The flashing lights of the cruisers driven by the deputies greeted Judith at the intersection of State Highway 19 and County W. She slowed to pull over in front of the first of seven, hoping Dani had alerted them to watch for her. Jumping out of her car, she ran over and leaned into the driver's side window of the first patrol car. "I'm Judith. You're to follow me," she said to the deputy driving.

"Got it," he said. "Dani Wright radioed us to follow you. We're ready. How far down the county road do you think it is?"

"About four miles. I'll slow down as I get closer. I was walking in there the other day, so I know about where I'm going, but the logging road isn't marked."

"Getting dark by the minute. Need a good light?" asked the deputy, jerking his thumb toward a colleague sitting beside him. "He can ride with you if that'll help."

"Yes," said Judith with enthusiasm. "Great idea."

The other deputy jumped out of the car and hurried over to climb in with Judith.

"Name is Jerry," he said as he held up a large torch-light. "You tell me when to turn this on. It works great along the roadside, shows light a good hundred yards."

The two of them, leaning forward to watch the road, drove in silence as Judith watched the mileage. When she had reached a point she knew was less than a mile away, she slowed. One mailbox went by, then the driveway to a small mobile home. They passed the shell of a broken-down barn, and she slowed even more. "Jerry, I'd use that torch now," she said to the man sitting beside her.

He was right. The sumac and tall grass running along-side the road were lit up nearly brighter than daylight. At an old post from the abandoned farm, Judith slowed down even more, pulling her car so close to the ditch that Jerry yelped, "Careful."

"It's okay," she said, pulling her steering wheel hard right to swing into a narrow dirt lane. She felt her SUV rattling down the logging lane and wondered, briefly, how badly the car would be scratched. She shrugged, thinking the scars would be well worth it.

Young poplars and balsams crowded the lane. "When was the last time anyone drove this?" asked Jerry under his breath. "Some of our cruisers are gonna need bodywork."

Judith threw him a grim smile. In her rearview mirror, she could see the flashing lights of the other deputies close behind. She knew the old lane ended in a wooded area near Hemlock Lake. She hoped that if she stopped there and had the deputies move to cover the distance from the county road to that point, they would be in position to see Ray and Lew when they emerged from the pine forest.

Judith parked and walked back to check with Jerry's partner in the first of the cruisers, which was right behind her.

"I'm about to check with Dani Wright, who is watching Sheriff Ferris's tracker, so we'll have an update on her position," she said. "But my instructions from her were to have you guys fan out along this logging lane. We can't be sure where she and Ray Pradt will come out, but they will need backup when they do. There is a chance that man they're searching for could come out first. If he does, he has to be stopped. He's not just a crook; he has killed a person."

With that, Jerry and his partner hurried to instruct the other deputies, starting at the rear, so the cars could back up with enough distance between each vehicle. The blockade was in place within minutes.

Judith's phone trilled. She pulled it from her jacket pocket and glanced at the caller's name before answering. "Yes, Dani, what?"

"Lew and Ray are getting close to Matt. I see their trackers maybe a third of a mile from the guy. His tracker isn't moving. I texted Lew that he may be hurt or resting or who knows. But they're close."

"How do we look?" asked Judith, knowing Dani could see her tracker on-screen. "I got the deputies covering this logging road, so I hope I got everyone in the right place."

"You're good, I think," said Dani. "You look to be just north of Brinkerhoff. I'll text Lew that if they reach him and move in the direction they're going now, they won't be far from you. Let's hope . . ."

"Yeah, let's hope," said Judith into the phone after Dani had clicked off.

Chapter
Forty-Two

∾

Pushing at branches of pine needles while keeping her eyes on Ray's back, Lew kept close behind him. Though night had fallen, her eyes had adjusted so well that she had no need of the head lamp. A late August moon shone through the treetops, making it easier to see.

Ray, too, had turned off his head lamp with its distracting beacon of light.

The forest felt reborn in the dark, with the air humid and warm, not hot; the trees pale gray and easy to see in the lingering twilight. Nor was the forest silent. Owls hooted overhead, two loons called to one another far off, and there was so much chattering that Lew knew the squirrels and chipmunks were alerting their families and friends to the presence of humans.

What she didn't hear was any sound from the man they were after. "Hold on, Ray," she said in a low voice after they had been trudging a while through the woods, trying to avoid tree stumps and half-rotten trunks of fallen birches. "I want to check with Dani, see how close we are to Brinkerhoff's tracker."

"Can't be too far," said Ray. "The tracks I see show him walking in the direction of the moon. Too bad. I wish he'd start going in circles again. If he would accommodate us, we could catch up with him in a few minutes."

Ray's wry humor worked.

"Don't we wish," said Lew.

She understood his frustration. After leaving Sarah and the EMT crew, they had gone back to where Ray could see Matt Brinkerhoff had run into the pine forest thinking he'd find Sarah Hatch. After an hour of tracking the man, Ray and Lew realized it wouldn't make sense, once they caught up with him, to backtrack. They were too far in.

Dani answered Lew's call immediately. Before Lew could ask her question, Dani said, "Yes, Judith has your deputies lined up along the logging road, which isn't too far from where you're at right now."

"But where is Brinkerhoff?"

Before Dani could answer, Ray waved an arm at Lew, signaling her to be quiet. Lew clicked off, hoping Dani would know not to call back.

She waited. Then she saw what Ray saw.

Like a giant pale-gray mushroom, Matt Brinkerhoff's white-blond head of hair shone in the moonlight. Through the trees, they could see him moving forward with what looked like a broken tree limb in one hand.

Ray stepped over a downed tree trunk and reached back to give Lew a hand over. They weren't more than twenty feet from the man. Standing side by side, Lew looked up at Ray, then moved forward, saying, "Drop the branch, Brinkerhoff. You're under arrest."

"What?" The man spun around. "Who's there? What are you talking about? I'm lost, for God's sake. Please help me."

Lew walked closer, her Sig Sauer pistol in her hand. Still wearing his business-casual khaki pants and an open-necked blue plaid shirt with the sleeves rolled up to his elbows, he would have appeared to be out for a walk, except his shirt had pulled loose from the pants, which had knees dark with dirt. He must have fallen or scrambled on all fours at some point. He was a sweaty mess with dark circles under his armpits.

"Drop the branch and put your hands up," said Lew, repeating herself as she and Ray walked up to the man.

He stared at her, at first not comprehending what she was saying. As it dawned on him, she saw fear in his eyes. Ray was holding his flashlight on the man, causing him to blink rapidly. When he could focus on Lew, the expression on the man's face told her what he was thinking: he was caught, he was afraid. *He is a coward*, she thought.

"Do you have any water?" he asked. "Please, some water?"

"In a moment," said Lew. "I'm Sheriff Lewellyn Ferris, and this is my deputy, Ray Pradt—"

"It's not my fault," said Matt, choking out his words. "The market for my companies tanked. My investors got scared. *None of it is my fault.*" He was sobbing.

"Matthew Brinkerhoff, I'm arresting you for the murder of Margaret Hanson."

The man blinked, her words clearly taking him aback. "Wh-a-a-t? Who the hell is that?"

"The sixteen-year-old girl you assaulted in July 1967 when you were a counselor at Camp Ashwabagon. A DNA sample recovered from her body at the time of the autopsy has shown a match to the DNA you provided after a stop for an apparent DUI two summers ago."

"But . . but . . . I wasn't the only guy there," he said, stammering. "And how could you know . . ." He didn't finish.

At that moment, the sound of a helicopter could be heard approaching overhead. The three of them glanced up simultaneously, though Lew made sure to keep an eye on the man in front of her.

"Now who can that be?" asked Matt.

"I believe that would be federal agent Steve Briscoe and federal agent Brian Pokorny. They're planning to arrest you for embezzlement and money laundering. You'll meet them later.

"And you'll get water when we reach the road, which isn't far. Now please hand over your cell phone."

Matt turned his eyes back to her. For a moment he didn't react, and then he reached into a rear pocket for an iPhone, which he handed over to Ray.

"Now please put your hands behind you," said Lew, walking around Matt to handcuff the man.

"I can't walk with these on," he said, as she began to cuff him.

"You'll do fine. Follow Ray. If you fall, we'll help you up."

"I want my lawyer," he said, with a trace of the arrogance Lew had encountered plenty of times with wealthy people who had never expected to be handcuffed or arrested.

"Sure. Later," said Lew. "Right now I want to get us out of the woods before the mosquitoes arrive." With Ray leading, they started to move north.

A scream pierced the air. "Who the hell is that?" asked Matt in a frightened voice. He stopped to look around anxiously.

"Oh, just a great horned owl tearing off the head of a rabbit," said Ray, his tone dry.

Matt winced. "Oh. I know how that feels," he said.

"I doubt that you do," said Lew. No one spoke again until they saw bright lights moving in the distant trees.

The helicopter hovered overhead too, with the wide beam of its searchlight making the way forward easier. The other lights turned out to be from the deputies, whose torches had been searching through the trees since Dani had alerted them that Sheriff Ferris and Ray would be emerging with their prisoner at any moment.

Chapter
Forty-Three

With Matt Brinkerhoff in front of them, Lew and Ray pushed their way out of the stand of young poplar trees and onto the logging road in front of the deputies. The entire area was lit with the bright blue and red flashing lights on their cars. Just as Lew turned Brinkerhoff over to one of the deputies to be moved to the McBride County Jail for arraignment in the morning, a squad car belonging to the Loon Lake Police Department pulled up.

"Sheriff Ferris, is everything okay?" asked Officer Todd Donovan, running toward her. "Steve and Brian know that you've got Brinkerhoff, and they would like to meet you and Matt Brinkerhoff back in your office. It's nearly ten o'clock and you have to be exhausted, but they insist." He sounded apologetic. "I'm here to give you a ride back to your office."

"No, thank you, I'm fine, I've got a ride," said Lew after a quick look down the road to confirm Judith had not left. "Do you mind giving Ray a ride home? He's been with me all day. He deserves a medal." She gave Ray a hug and nudged him toward Todd.

After confirming that Matt Brinkerhoff was in the company of two of her deputies and on the way back to town, Lew walked down the logging road to where a dark figure was leaning against an SUV.

"Judith," she said as she neared the car. "Mind giving this hitchhiker a ride to town?"

"I might fit you in," said Judith, half laughing, half crying. "You must know how I feel. I never thought this night would come."

"Oh, I can only imagine," said Lew. "But I've been worried about you ever since I heard that DNA sample was a match to Matt Brinkerhoff."

"What—you thought I'd might do something crazy?"

"No, but I wasn't sure how you would react. How do you feel?"

"Let me ask you a couple of questions first," said Judith.

"I'll try to answer, but keep in mind I'm no lawyer."

"First, do you think he will still be charged with murder even though it's been so long since my sister's death?"

"Without question. There's no statute of limitations on murder. Considering the circumstances, I have no doubt he will go to trial, be convicted, and serve the rest of his life in prison."

"What about the federal charges for the embezzlement and money laundering?"

"Five years, maybe. Five years plus life. Judith, the man is seventy-three years old. He is going to die in prison."

Judith drove in silence with Lew watching her face through the shadows thrown by oncoming traffic. "How do you feel about that?" Lew asked.

"Satisfied. Just . . . satisfied."

They rode quietly for a while, headlights illuminating the path ahead, until Judith spoke again.

"The person who will be happy with all this is my daughter," she said. "She has accused me of being obsessed about my sister's death, and she's been right—I couldn't let it go. I knew she hadn't died in an accident and that someone was responsible for taking her life."

Judith turned to Lew with a half smile as she said, "But now that's over. I can live a normal life. No more nightmares."

Chapter
Forty-Four

It was two in the morning when Lew pulled into Osborne's driveway. Mallory was sound asleep in her downstairs bedroom, but Osborne was in the kitchen pulling a grilled cheese off the broiler.

"Sit down, Lewellyn, you must be famished." He set out a glass of milk beside the sandwich.

"Do you believe I forgot to eat? Haven't had a thing since lunchtime," she said between bites as she inhaled the sandwich.

Taking the chair beside her, Osborne gave her a soft smile. "I was hoping you would remember tonight is one of my nights. But I would understand if you needed to be in your own bed."

"Doc"—she gave him the dim eye—"my bed is your bed and vice versa." Then, in a sober tone, she said, "I find it hard to understand how we could be looking at two people from the same family committing such heinous crimes. I mean, I understand Matt Brinkerhoff and his money laundering, embezzling from his own company. Obviously the guy is one of those men who think they're smarter than everyone. But it's what he did years ago.

"Doc, his own son, too. Both of them assaulting women like they did. Where does that come from? It's like a cancer in the family."

"I know," said Osborne. "I've seen it before too. Almost a genetic predisposition. But my personal theory is that people, parents in particular, forget that children learn good and bad behavior from the adults around them. Who knows how Matt treated his son? Did he approve when the kid bullied other kids? Kicked the family dog? Did the boy see him mistreat his wives? No one knows."

The two of them sat there quietly while Lew finished gulping down her milk.

"Ready for bed?" Osborne asked her.

"Kind of. I still feel the adrenaline pulsing through me. Thank God for Ray and his instinct in those pines. There were times when I thought we'd have to get out the forest service to find us."

After climbing into bed, Lew curled up next to Osborne. She lay there.

"Are you asleep, Doc?"

"Not yet. I've been thinking how remarkable it was that Bruce was able to find the right people and a lab that could restore the DNA sample that was saved in Dr. Nystrom's evidence slides so long ago.

"You know, Lew, when I think about it, it was Roger Nystrom working from the grave who really nailed Matt Brinkerhoff. Don't you agree?"

"I do. Can we go to sleep now?"

Lew turned over on her side. A loon called in the distance. She would be happy if she could get three hours of sleep.

"Seriously, it's one thing to get a DNA match today. You got the science, the databases . . ."

"Doc. Please, sleep."

"I know, I know."

Lew turned toward him and laid an arm across his chest. "Dr. Nystrom's work has been critical, but only because you remembered what he had done. If you hadn't recalled how he was so careful with his evidence and if you hadn't urged Bruce to search for those files . . ."

She lifted her head to give him a quick kiss. "Dr. Paul Osborne, I'm fortunate that your memory is as good as those ancient dental files of yours."

"You really think so?" He sounded like a happy teenager.

"Sleep."

Chapter
Forty-Five

When Lew got to the parking lot in the morning, she had four television and newspaper reporters waiting. She recognized two who would have driven up from Wausau to cover the news.

"Please, folks," she said, before walking into the building, "I can't speak with you right now. I have an arraignment this morning, and after that I'll be happy to share what details are available."

"Sheriff Ferris, we just spoke with the federal agents," said one of the reporters. "They said Matthew Brinkerhoff may have embezzled as much as five hundred million dollars. Is that correct?"

"I'll have details later," said Lew, repeating herself. "Two o'clock today, I'll hold a press conference. Until then, I have a busy, busy morning. Please excuse me."

She escaped to her office, where half a dozen people were waiting. "I'm Matthew Brinkerhoff's lawyer,

Sheriff Ferris," said a tall, dark-haired man. Flew in this morning—"

"Fine. See you in court at eleven," said Lew, shutting him down. Off in one corner stood Martha Burns, the attorney for the Knudsen family. She waved, and Lew walked over to her. "Why are you here? Did something change with Barry Brinkerhoff?"

"Yes," said Martha, her demeanor calm. "I thought you would appreciate knowing that I've been able to move that case to Tomahawk County. No more interference from Judge Voelker. I wanted you to know that so there can be a request made during today's arraignment to move the senior Brinkerhoff's trial to the same venue, Tomahawk County. I've alerted the district attorney, so that should happen no matter what Matthew Brinkerhoff's attorney says."

"Thank you, Martha, that is good news," said Lew.

After Martha left, Lew walked over to the two men sitting at the conference table under the tall windows at the far end of the room. They looked exhausted. "Steve and Brian, good morning," said Lew, sitting down beside them. "I can't thank you enough for your help last night."

"Don't kid us, Sheriff Ferris," said Steve. "We got there so late. You and your deputies had it covered."

Lew nodded; she knew the men felt they'd messed up. But their intentions were good. "Gentlemen, that search-light that you worked from that helicopter last night is what saved us. Ray and I had Brinkerhoff in cuffs and we had the light from our head lamps, but we needed that light. Bet you we'd have been out there another hour if you hadn't shown up."

Their expressions eased a little.

"We have good news this morning," said Brian. "Our agents stopped that van up near Manitowish Waters right on Highway 51. Also, looks like Canadian authorities have located more of the stolen art in a warehouse up in Ontario. We need to let Sarah Hatch know."

"You sure do," said Lew, getting to her feet. "I want the two of you to join me for a press conference at two o'clock today. We'll hold it in my office, and feel free to answer questions. But I have to warn you that you may be overshadowed with news that I have."

"We know already," said Steve. "Dani Wright told us this morning that you got Brinkerhoff for murder on a cold case from the sixties. Right?"

"Darn that Dani," said Lew with a smile. "She never can keep a secret."

Hurrying past two reporters who insisted on hanging out in the hallway, Lew made her way to Dani's office. Dani and Judith had just arrived and were settling in at their desks.

"Dani, thank you again for your hard work last night. Without your updates on everyone's whereabouts, my investigation would never have succeeded."

Dani looked happy.

"She's brilliant," said Judith, "and she was here until after midnight—"

"Couldn't have done it without your help, Judith," said Dani.

"She's right," said Lew. "With the two of you organizing the deputies the way you did, the operation could not have gone more smoothly. I want you both to check your schedules, as I want to give you extra personal days. You deserve it." And she left the room, leaving two pleased employees smiling at each other.

Matt Brinkerhoff was arraigned at eleven that morning. The charges included sexual assault and murder of a juvenile, embezzling, and money laundering. He was returned to jail with bail denied, due to the likelihood that he had the means and motive to flee the country.

His lawyer was furious.

The reporters waiting for the press conference were astounded when they heard the murder charges. All four hit their cell phones to instruct their colleagues to unearth news stories from the archives of their various news organizations.

Chapter
Forty-Six

Late that afternoon, when the last of the reporters left her office, Lew pushed back from her desk, letting her shoulders slump with fatigue. She had had it. The last thing she wanted to do was handle the current file staring at her: the file demanding the details of her firing of Deer Haven chief of police Alan Stern. She had to write up the details of his firing for submission to the county board. She pushed the file away, deciding to tackle it the next morning.

A knock on the door prompted her to wonder why no one had alerted her to a visitor. It had to be someone she knew. She relaxed, saying, "Come in."

Mallory walked in, followed by Sarah Hatch, who was wearing a large, soft cast on her right leg. "Do you have a minute for us to say good-bye?" asked Mallory.

"Of course. Come and take a chair, you two. Sarah, are you doing okay?"

"Quite nicely, though I am a little tired," said Sarah, letting herself down into the chair carefully.

"She's catching a flight back to New York City early tomorrow morning," said Mallory, "and spending the night at Dad's with us."

"Good," said Lew. "Steve and Brian told me this morning that their agents were able to stop that van and have also found more of the art stored up in Ontario. Does that help with your gallery's situation?"

"Certainly does," said Sarah. "I talked with my husband late last night about it, and he assured me that the insurance my father arranged for our gallery years ago should help to cover some of the losses."

"Maybe you didn't need to fly out here after all?" asked Lew.

"Not sure about that. The art I thought I had sold Matt Brinkerhoff is worth millions of dollars. I'll be meeting with agents for the Treasury Department next week to go over what he stole and where matters sit, but there is very good news. Because the federal authorities have gotten involved, my gallery won't be accused of being a party to Matt Brinkerhoff's money-laundering scheme.

"Even better, people from the auction houses and other galleries with whom I do business have been reaching out, offering to help me." She gave a slight smile. "There is a silver lining after all."

"And you are alive, not eaten by bears in the big woods."

Sarah laughed with relief. "And I am alive, thanks to you and that wonderful Ray Pradt. Thank you, Sheriff Ferris."

"And I thank you, Lew," said Mallory, getting up from her chair. "I am still amazed at how deep a hole Matt Brinkerhoff has dug. My job over the next few months will be to try to keep our PR firm from losing money on the projects we were involved in with that man and his hedge fun. Here's hoping we don't take too great a financial hit. Anyway, I'll be driving back to Chicago tomorrow."

She walked over to give Lew a hug. "See you next trip and hope it is a quiet one," she said with a laugh.

Chapter
Forty-Seven

Her energy restored after a good night's sleep, Lew arrived at her office with a list of priorities she was determined to conquer. Though she knew she was making headway, her desk was still cluttered with too much unfinished business.

First, she needed to write and email her memo on the firing of Alan Stern to the chairman of the McBride County board. She hit send. Good, that was done.

Now she needed to fill the vacant position of chief of the Loon Lake Police. She joined Dani in the office the woman shared with Judith to get the basics underway.

"Here is a copy of the posting we have to make," she said, handing over a copy of one she had found in the file from when her predecessor had hired Alan Stern.

She glanced at Dani, who was reviewing the posting Lew had handed her. "Okay," said Dani, "this looks good. I'll arrange for applicants to send résumés to me."

"Good," said Lew, "let's see what we get over the next week, because I know who I want to hire for that position."

Dani gave her a questioning look.

"Officer Donovan. He's been on the force for eight years, and I have always been able to depend on the man. I know I'm required to post the opening, and I will take a good look at who applies, but I plan to recommend Todd Donovan immediately after the week is up. All we will need then is approval from the Loon Lake City Council. I'm sure Todd Donovan will be happy to move into the position.

"And I have one more posting for you to handle. Deer Haven chief of police. I understand from the city's personnel office and all the paperwork concerning Alan Stern's termination"—Lew made it a point not to use the word *firing*—"that I am now authorized to fill that position too."

She looked at Dani. "We have busy days ahead, don't we?"

Dani gave a happy shrug. Lew knew she was happier being busy than she was when she was bored.

"I posted the opening already—well. Kind of," said Dani in a self-satisfied tone.

"You did?" Lew was taken aback. Sitting nearby and listening to the two of them, Judith tried to hide a smile. Dani was good, always one step ahead of her boss.

"Last week I got a call from a police officer with ten years' experience in law enforcement over in the Fox Valley region. He heard about Stern's leaving, and he loves to ice fish. His application will be emailed in sometime later this week," said Dani. "I told him to wait until you told me we could post the position."

"Let's hope he looks as good on paper as his tip-ups," said Lew. "And what about you?" she asked, turning to Judith. "What do we do with you? I can't imagine you want to keep working here now that we've solved your sister's case."

Of course this was something that had crossed Judith's mind—after all, that was the primary reason she had taken this job. But she had found that she enjoyed the work, and she enjoyed being back in Loon Lake without the shadow of her sister's unsolved death.

"Are you kidding?" Judith responded. "What else am I going to do? Go fishing?"

Lew smiled. "There are worse ways to spend your retirement," she said.

"Yes, there are. And I do plan to fish," said Judith. "In fact, I've signed up to fly east for one of those long weekends of classes at the Wulff School of Fly Fishing. Just what you recommended.

"But, seriously, Lew, I find working here to be interesting, challenging, and sometimes downright fascinating. And it's work that helps people who are going through hard times. If you'll let me assist Dani but also work those cold cases with the Wausau boys—"

"Are you sure?" asked Lew, sounding hopeful as she interrupted Judith. "Because that would take a burden off my shoulders. And we could work those together."

"With your permission, I'll pull the data on a couple cases," said Judith, "and then we can go over it to see what direction you and Bruce Peters want to take."

What Judith didn't say was that the job was her ticket to a new Loon Lake, a town that no longer harbored grief and suspicion, a town that was now truly home. And her parents' house had been transformed too. It no longer hid secrets. It had become the safe haven she remembered from childhood, from before her sister's death.

"It's a plan," said Lew, ready to get back to her desk. As she stood up, she stopped to put a hand on Judith's shoulder. "Doc and I decided earlier that this may be a perfect evening for a late-summer hatch. Care to join us on the Prairie River this evening?"

"Try to stop me. I'll ride your back fender if I have to," said Judith with a grin.

Lew's cell phone rang. She answered, listened, and turned to Dani and Judith with a smile. "They've finished the renovations on our offices in the McBride County Sheriff's Department. We can move in Monday."

Back in her office, Lew turned to her next item. She had a person in mind to replace Todd on the Loon Lake police force. He would have to approve, of course, if he accepted the position of Loon Lake police chief, but she thought she had a darn good candidate for him to consider.

Just before Lew was elected sheriff, a young woman fresh out of the community college's law enforcement program had applied to the Loon Lake Police Department. A single mother who had scored high in all her classes and training, she reminded Lew of herself twenty years earlier. It would be the new police chief's decision to make, but Lew had a good feeling about the candidate.

Chapter Forty-Eight

∽

After unloading their gear from Lew's pickup, Osborne pulled on his waders and was about to step into the stream when Lew stopped him.

"The wind from the southwest today will be perfect for working on your double haul, Doc."

"Not sure about that," said Osborne. "Every time I try it, I screw up. I've decided I can catch trout just fine without it. *Perfect* is the enemy of *good enough*."

"Oh, come on. You'll get the hang of it," said Lew. "I watched you the other day, and all you need to work on is that back cast. Be sure your line hand pulls the line in on the power snap, then gives it back while the line is unrolling backward."

"Easy to say." Doc sounded glum, and he started to wade forward, heading upstream.

"I know, I know, but all you have to remember is your hauling arm shouldn't stiffen at the end of your hauling move—but keep it flexed."

"That's all?" He still sounded doubtful.

"Okay, try it right now."

With reluctance, Osborne got himself into position in the middle of the stream, raised his right arm, and cast, saying to himself, "*Pull* and give back, *pull* and give back."

Applause greeted his ears, and he turned in surprise. "I did it?"

"You did, Doc. Beautiful," said Lew with a wide grin as she clapped her hands.

Happy in his heart, Osborne started upstream.

Lew turned to Judith, who had waded in behind her. "Ready?" she asked as she studied the cloud of insects hovering over the water, "This is great, Judith. We've got a nice blue-winged olive hatch this evening. Now," she said, "show me which trout fly you should use."

Judith studied the box of trout flies that Lew was holding. She chose one.

"Yes, that Royal Wulff number sixteen should work. Good choice. Let's give it a try, and I'll coach your casting."

* * *

An hour and one brook trout caught and released later, the two women sat down among the boulders crowding the riverbank to relax and wait for Osborne.

"I think you'll really like the Wulff fly-fishing school," said Lew as she shared her trail mix. "It'll be three days of hard work, but you'll know casting and stream science when you're done. One nice feature is the ponds they use for casting lessons. That helps make the learning process so easy, but they take you into the river too. Who knows? You may even catch a trout." Lew sat back, crossing her legs and feeling relaxed for the first time in days.

"I can't wait," said Judith. "I plan to make my flight reservations tomorrow. I'm hoping they can sell me a new fly rod. A *good* fly rod, one like yours. Didn't you tell me that's where you got yours?" she asked.

"Yes," said Lew. "I bought it when I was out there. It's one Joan Wulff designed for Winston rods. Works great for me."

"I'm enjoying fly-fishing more than I ever expected," said Judith, "so I want to invest in the right gear."

"While you're at the Wulff school, you'll be able to try numerous rods. You'll be surprised how easy it'll be to find a fly rod that feels like an extension of your arm, of your entire body," said Lew. "It'll cost a few pennies, but it's worth it. You'll also learn more about trout flies, enough that you can decide if you want to 'tie 'em or buy 'em,' as they say." Lew grinned.

"What do you do, Lew?"

"I do both. And friends give me trout flies too. What I think is important as you get into this sport is deciding how technical you want to be. And that is a personal choice. You can bury yourself in the life cycles of insects and the challenges of tying perfect trout flies or swing loose with the simplicity of Japanese tenkara."

"Slow down," said Judith. "I haven't heard that word before. Tenkara? What is that?"

"A very, very stripped-down version of fly-fishing. Many people swear by it. If you're interested, I have a book about it that I'll lend you. But take your time, Judith. You want to choose what makes *you* happy in the water."

They sat quiet, munching on the trail mix.

"I can't tell you how happy I am that you arrested that man for the murder of my sister."

"Would never have happened if Doc and Bruce Peters hadn't found Dr. Nystrom's files and those slides. That DNA match is what nailed Brinkerhoff. Not me."

"And what matters to me is that after all these years, he has to pay for what he did."

"He will. He's facing life in prison."

"Good. I want him to think about what he did every day for the rest of his miserable life."

"And he will," said Lew. After a long pause, she said, "Do you mind if I change the subject?"

"Only if it involves fish," said Judith with a smile as she wiped away a stray tear. Lew could see she had decided to leave the past behind and move on . . . into the Prairie River. Not a bad place to start.

Chapter Forty-Nine

Later that evening and before going to bed, Judith made a decision.

First, she called Kate. "Hi, hon, sorry to call so late," she said, hearing her daughter's drowsy voice. "But I want you to know, I've decided to drive down this weekend and take a good look at that condo."

She could hear rustling as Kate sat up in her bed. "Really, Mom? I think you'll love it. I'll get us an appointment with the realtor."

"What I will love is being close to you and the kids. But I'm only going to be down there on weekends. I'm keeping my job here."

"Why? You don't need the money. You don't need to—"

"Keep obsessing over my family tragedy? I know. But Kate, I've always worked, and I like the people I'm working with up here." She paused for a moment, then said, "And I have a new obsession . . ."

"Mom," said her daughter, warning in her voice. "What are you up to now?"

"I'm learning to fly-fish. I've taken a few lessons, and I love it."

Judith could sense her daughter's relief before she spoke. "Oh, okay," said Kate with a sigh. "At least it's healthy."

"I'll tell you more tomorrow. Good night, sweetheart."

Hmm, thought Judith, after hanging up, *maybe I'll invite Kate to come along to the Wulff school with me. That would be a good mother-daughter trip. Yes, I'll give that a try.*

*   *   *

After the call to her daughter, Judith walked down the hallway to her sister's bedroom. The door was closed. She paused for a long moment, thinking, then opened it.

Her parents had not changed a thing since the night they'd learned that Maggie would never be coming home. Her bed was made with the peach-and-white quilt her grandmother had given her when she turned thirteen. The tiny stuffed owl she had loved since she was five was still snuggled against white pillows.

The closet held her clothes: her prom dress and even her purple-and-white cheerleading skirt from her sophomore year. The oak dresser drawers were full of socks and T-shirts, underwear and pajamas.

Judith smiled to herself as she touched the items before closing the drawers. Sitting on the bed, she knew the time had come to make a plan. Over the next weekend, she would empty the closet and drawers and donate the clothing to St. Mary's Thrift Shop, which benefited the homeless. Then she would call a local woman who handled estate sales and work with her to decide what to do with her sister's furniture and perhaps some of the other furnishings. It was time to move on. Perhaps she would redecorate the room for her grandchildren to use on visits, and one of the bedrooms for Kate or other guests.

She looked over at the small maple desk beside the bed. She pulled open the top drawer. She didn't need a key. Maggie had had no reason to lock her desk. After all, she had been planning to be home by eleven, her curfew set by their parents, and tumble into bed. Judith gazed down at the bright-blue cover of the diary that Maggie had kept in the top drawer, an easy reach from her bed.

Judith opened it to the last entry. It had been written on a Wednesday, two days before Maggie's death. She had been excited to have met a handsome junior camp counselor. He wanted to pick her up Friday to go with him to a party.

He is so cute, she had written, *but I have to tell Mom and Dad I'm going over to Colleen's house. He can pick me up there.*

Judith knew what that was about: her parents had not wanted Maggie going out with boys they didn't know. Judith reached for one of the pens her sister had kept in the drawer beside the diary.

Just below Maggie's last entry, Judith wrote the current date and a few words. Then she sat back against the bed pillows and read what she had written.

Dear Maggie,

All is good. Sleep well.

Love,

Judith

And with those words, Judith embraced the peace for which she had been searching since she was eight years old.

Enjoyed the read?

We'd love to hear your thoughts!

crookedlanebooks.com/feedback

Acknowledgments

A heartfelt thank-you to everyone who has helped make *Hidden in the Pines* read well and look good. This includes Ben LeRoy, my good friend and editor, who is generous with excellent advice; Sara J. Henry, with her impeccable editing; and Nicole Lecht, who designed the lovely, haunting cover. But none of this could have occurred without meticulous guidance from Melissa Rechter, assistance from Madeline Rathle and Dulce Botello, and the efforts of everyone on the Crooked Lane team—production and marketing—who have helped make *Hidden in the Pines* possible.

You make me look good.